THE SINNER'S BIBLE

THE SINNER'S BIBLE

A Natalie Brandon Thriller

Jenni Wiltz

Decanter Press
PILOT HILL, CALIFORNIA

Published in the United States by Decanter Press.
For information, contact:
publisher@enniwiltz.com

Publisher's Cataloging-in-Publication Data
Wiltz, Jenni.
The sinner's bible / Jenni Wiltz.
132 p. ; 22 cm.
ISBN 978-1-942348-14-6 (pbk)
ISBN 978-1-942348-13-9 (eBook)
1. Great Britain — Kings and Rulers — Fiction.
2. Queens — Great Britain — Fiction.
3. Suspense fiction. 4. Historical fiction. I. Title.
PS3623.I48S56 2017
813'.6 — dc23
Library of Congress Control Number: 2017902098

For Sara

Stuart Family Tree

JAMES I: 1566 - 1625
Married: Anne of Denmark
Children: Elizabeth, Charles I

CHARLES I: 1600 – 1649
Married: Henrietta Maria, daughter of Henri IV
Children: Charles II, James II, Henriette

HENRIETTE ("MINETTE"): 1644 - 1670
Married: Philippe, duc d'Orléans
Children: Marie Louise d'Orléans, Anne Marie d'Orléans

CHARLES II: 1630 - 1685
Married: Catherine of Braganza
Children: no legitimate children

JAMES II: 1633 – 1701
Married: Anne Hyde (1); Mary of Modena (2)
Children: Mary II, Anne, James Francis Edward

MARY II: 1662 - 1694
Married: William of Orange
Children: no children

ANNE: 1665 - 1714
Married: George of Denmark
Children: no surviving children

CHAPTER ONE

William Laud, the Bishop of London, clutched a small book to his chest. He spread his palms over the cover, as if he could blot out its existence by hiding it from view.

There was no fire in the grate.

He shivered as he stood before the double doors of the presence chamber. The men-at-arms on either side stared straight ahead, giving no indication of the king's mood…or how willing they were to carry out an order to kill the bringer of bad tidings.

He closed his eyes and wondered how much longer Charles would make him wait.

How could this have happened? he wondered. How could so many people have seen it and said nothing? It had been a year. An entire bloody year, without a word from anyone.

Either God had blinded them to it, or they had become estranged from Him, setting aside His word. No matter how he couched it in his mind, it boded ill for himself and for England.

God was testing them, and they had failed for an entire year.

But what threat was He warning them against? It had been twenty-six years since the Jesuit Treason. Digby, Wintour, Fawkes, and the lot of them were rotting in their nameless graves. Princess Elizabeth, the girl they would have made queen, had been shipped off to Bohemia. James I, the king they would have murdered, had instead brought the world the most holy translation of the Bible ever wrought by man.

That should have been the end of it.

But it was not.

Because King James's son had married a Papist.

Since the death of Buckingham, she'd become Charles's sole confidant and advisor. She, with her sloe eyes and soft voice, who could barely speak English seven years after her arrival. She who kept her own confessor and chapel and flaunted them before his eyes.

William sighed. Was this how it began? The slow slide into Papal dominion? First the queen, then the royal children, then perhaps the whole kingdom when her son, a second Charles, ascended the throne. All that Good Queen Bess had hoped to preserve by murdering her Catholic cousin Mary, Queen of Scots would be torn away from them again.

The gallows or the stake, he wondered. Which would it be for him?

The presence chamber's doors flew open and the men-at-arms stamped their halberds as King Charles I passed into the antechamber. The queen followed him, swathed in pearls and a fox-fur wrap. William bowed low as the king and queen swept toward him. "Your Majesties," he said.

"William," Charles replied warmly. "What brings you here on such a cold day? I'd have thought the warmth of your hearth would suit you better than this drafty old place."

The king spoke French, as he always did in the queen's presence, requiring him to reply in kind. "My duty suits me in any weather, Your Majesty."

"And what is your duty today?"

His hands shook as he held out the book. "The devil is at work in England, sire."

Charles glanced at the book, with the words *Holy Bible* stamped on the cover. "Looks to be the opposite," he said.

The dark-haired queen leaned over Charles's shoulder. "Your father's translation?"

Charles nodded. "A new printing, is it not, Laud?"

"Yes, Your Majesty, commissioned last year in the house of Barker and Lucas."

"We placed the order, they printed it," Charles said. "What do you wish me to do with it now?"

"Please take it, Your Majesty," he begged. "Open to the page I have marked."

Charles took the book from his shaking hand. A red ribbon marked a page near the beginning, and the king thumbed straight to it.

He watched the sovereign's face as he read the small type. He could have done more to draw the king's attention to the passage, but he wanted to see how it happened, how the awareness dawned on him.

The queen read over Charles's shoulder. It was her eyes that fell upon the abomination first, proving she had a better grasp of their language than she had led anyone to believe. She gasped and held a hand to her mouth.

A moment later, Charles found it. His face, normally soft and expressive, hardened like the effigies in Westminster Abbey. "How many?"

"I do not know, Your Majesty."

"How long?"

William blinked. This was the moment he revealed how far the devil had made inroads into their kingdom and their church. "A year," he whispered.

"Unacceptable!" Charles thundered, tossing the book into the grate. "This is no Holy Bible! This is a jest, committed at my expense! How could they let this happen?"

"I do not—"

"Bring the printers to me, Laud. Escort them into the Star Chamber and let them tell me to my face why they have made a mockery of my father's achievement."

"Yes, Your Majesty," he said, lowering his head and taking one step back. Best to take Charles's command as a dismissal, lest there be a separate punishment in wait for him.

"Laud," Charles snapped.

He gulped. "Y—yes, Your Majesty?"

"Burn them," Charles said, his dark eyes alight with fury. "Burn them all."

CHAPTER TWO

*A*vi Druckman *slipped* on a respirator and a pair of vinyl gloves. The book in front of him wasn't particularly old or valuable in a scholarly sense, but the university had rules for this kind of thing. The book had been purchased at auction. They had only the seller's word that it had never been in a flood. Until he inspected it for himself, he'd have no idea what kind of mold might be present inside it. Once he made an assessment of its condition for the insurance paperwork, he was supposed to make a video of it for the library's Facebook page.

Avi sighed.

He'd earned bachelor's degrees in cultural anthropology and Jewish studies, and a master's in library science, but his main duty as Associate Librarian of the Rosemont University Rare Book & Manuscript Collection was to post stuff to

Facebook. *We'd really like you to be more active on Twitter,* the library's executive director had said. *Erik Kwakkel has ten times as many followers as we do. And what about Snapchat? I hear all the kids are on Snapchat.*

He made a mental note to dust off his resume after work.

Maybe Berkeley was hiring.

All his favorite Indian restaurants were in Berkeley.

His stomach growled and he envisioned a plate of murgh korma. "Why couldn't you have been a Gutenberg?" he said, glaring at the small, brown Bible in front of him.

Most old books were comforting. He loved the musty smell of dried calfskin and the tang of mildew. He found pleasure in the smoothness of vellum or the textured weave of rag-cotton linen. Nothing in real life shone as brightly as the carmine and malachite in Rabbi Kantrowitz's illuminated Bible, produced in medieval Spain decades before the Expulsion.

Other kids had hurried home from school, ready to pop another CD into the computer for ten free hours on AOL. He'd gone to Rabbi Kantrowitz's to run his fingers along the gilded spines of the old man's books.

But this book was different.

Its plainness was almost oppressive.

The cracked leather cover had peeled away from the boards. The spine and pages were in decent condition, with no visible water damage. He took notes on their appearance, then lifted the cover carefully.

He shivered as soon as he touched it.

There was nothing comforting about this particular book. Plus, it was all that stood between him and a plate of samosas.

He took hurried notes on the condition of the endbands and lifted the back cover. A few chips of desiccated leather fell onto the last page.

He squinted at them.

There was something on the page beneath them.

Handwriting, he thought. His eyes followed the loops and swirls of a fanciful script in faded black ink. "What do we have here?" he said, reaching for his magnifying glass.

Every librarian dreamed of finding something historically significant in the scholarly equivalent of a dumpster. Was this his moment? He licked his lips and held the magnifying glass over the faint cursive script.

"Show me what you got," he muttered, bending close over the page.

It was a list—a column of names.

His heart sank when he realized what it was.

An ordinary family had used what they thought was an ordinary Bible to record their births and deaths. They hadn't even done a good job. In fact, they'd sucked royally at it. There were no dates, so you couldn't even tell which was a birth and which was a death.

He put down the magnifying glass and sighed. What had he expected to find? An inscription from Ben Jonson? A dirty limerick from Milton?

It was useless.

Avi closed the book.

The Facebook video would have to wait until after lunch. His stomach was growling so loud that his phone's camera would capture his malnutrition for all posterity. He slid the book back onto one of the storage room's rolling metal shelves and stripped off his gloves.

Rajah's All-You-Can-Eat Indian Buffet was calling his name.

CHAPTER THREE

Ezra Hawkins cut the crust from his last slice of bread. He picked up the spatula and scraped the peanut butter jar as if he were giving it a clean, close shave. The bread tore as he spread the peanut butter onto it.

There was one banana left on the counter.

Spots covered its peel like a Rorschach test.

Every goddamn one looked like the amorphous blue splotches on Jacob's fMRI.

He sliced the banana and cut each slice into quarters. He chose the biggest piece and pushed it into the center of the peanut butter, representing an atom's nucleus. *Sodium,* he thought. One valence electron on top, one on the bottom. He pushed more banana pieces into the peanut butter to represent the second orbital—two electrons on top, two on bottom, two on the left, and two on the right.

He picked up the last piece of banana.

If he set it in the third orbital, he'd be depicting sodium's elemental form, a highly unstable metal. If that metal touched water, the last electron would cause a violent explosion. But if he ate that piece instead, he'd be left with a stable and harmless sodium ion.

Ezra looked out the window.

Drought had killed their corn and alfalfa. Relentless pumping of the aquifer had dropped their elevation by a foot in thirteen months. Now there was no more water to pump.

He pushed the banana into the peanut butter.

"Boom," he said.

§

HE HEARD JACOB'S truck before he saw it. The heater was making a weird noise that neither of them could fix. The irregular thumping sounded like a heartbeat, audible over the hum of the old Chevy's V-8 engine.

The heater, Ezra thought. *He's cold.*

He reached into the fridge for their last piece of ginger. It was cheaper at the Asian market, which meant he'd have to make another stop next time he went out. He grated a few thin shavings onto the sandwich. Probably not enough for thermogenesis, but it was the best he could do at the moment.

He set the sandwich on a plate.

The doctor had warned him about the things Jacob would start to lose: balance, appetite, memory, feeling in his arms and legs. But his brother still looked like the All-County linebacker who'd gone to the state quarterfinals a decade ago—thick neck, big arms, and thighs like tree trunks. The changes would happen fast, the doctor had said, like watching corn grow.

I don't remember what that looks like, he thought. Without water, cancer was the only thing that grew.

His brother opened the door to the double-wide.

"Boots off," Ezra said, sliding the plated sandwich down the counter. "I just swept."

Jacob ignored him, tossing a canvas bag onto the table. Then he peeled up the top slice of bread and frowned at the banana bits. "What's this one? A Picasso?"

"Electron diagram."

Jacob sat down and took a bite of the sandwich. "This tastes weird. What'd you do to it?"

"It's ginger. Supposed to make you warm."

Jacob chewed and swallowed. "There's a Stanford catalog in there."

"That's not what the money's for."

"It could be."

"No," he growled. "It couldn't." He picked up the canvas bag and shook its contents onto the table: letters, magazines, small parcels, and anything else the good mail carriers of Crows Landing had delivered to their intended recipients. "Did you switch license plates?"

"Give me a break."

"It was just a question."

"It's done," Jacob said, tilting his chair onto two legs. "I used the last one."

"Good thing license plates are a renewable resource." He plucked a long manila envelope from the pile and held it up. He'd started stealing mail to pay for groceries, but soon learned it was good for a hell of a lot more than that. A padded envelope full of cocaine had kept them afloat for three months. If he'd known the cartels were using the U.S. postal service to move product, he'd have started stealing mail years ago.

He began sorting the day's haul into piles: burn, cash, sell, keep. When he held up an issue of *Car and Driver*, Jacob reached for it immediately.

It took so little to make his brother happy, but it would take a lot more for him. The property tax on their land was four and a half years overdue. In six months, the tax collector could sell the farm at auction. He'd put everything they had into a new well, just in time for it to run dry. There had been nothing left when Jacob needed surgery. He'd paid for that by stealing cars, but even that wasn't enough anymore.

Genetic abnormality, the doctor had said. *Epidermal growth factor.*

The tumor had reappeared almost immediately after surgery. Jacob would be dead before summer unless he found a doctor willing to try a second operation on a stage 4 glioblastoma.

Where the hell was he supposed to find that doctor? Or get that kind of money?

Ezra pushed his hair out of his eyes. He had to think.

"You look like a surfer," Jacob said. "That dude in *Point Break*."

"He's dead."

"You gonna read that Stanford catalog?"

"No."

"Why not? You got something better to do today?"

"You're looking at it," he said, dropping a mail-in-rebate check into the keep pile.

Jacob finished the sandwich and licked his fingers. "Where to next, little brother?"

"The sink. Wash that plate."

"Can it sit?"

"I just did the goddamn dishes. I want an empty sink."

"The water's cold. I can't get warm after."

Ezra looked out the window to the propane tank. Their account had been delinquent so many times that the propane company wouldn't come unless he pre-paid for the fill-up. Every morning for two weeks now, he'd boiled a pot of water and dragged the bath mat next to the electric stove. They were out of propane. Out of food. After Jacob's last scan, he was almost out of hope.

"Shit." His fingers clutched the edge of the table. A splinter pierced the webbing of his right hand. "Shit, shit, shit, shit!"

He swept the pile of mail off the table.

"It's fine," Jacob said, setting his plate in the sink. "I'll do it."

"No. Go put my coat on." Jacob changed directions and plucked his puffer coat from the sofa. The sleeves hit two inches above his brother's wrists. "Hey princess," he said. "Don't forget the matching gloves."

Jacob reached out to ruffle his hair.

He ducked and batted his brother's hand away. "I hate it when you do that."

"I know."

"I mean I really hate it when you do that."

"I know." Jacob ran one hand over his shaved head, resting it on the back of his neck. "Just be glad you have hair, man. You don't miss it until it's gone."

"You want me to shave my head to prove you wrong? I will."

"Hey Ezra," Jacob said softly. "Thank you."

"Don't you say that. Not now."

"You rather I waited?"

He held his breath. The trailer was shrinking, closing in on him. Everywhere he looked, he saw reminders of the time his brother didn't have. The bills, the calendar, the magazine subscriptions with expiration dates further away than the doctors' best-case scenario. "Don't you thank me. All I did was make a sandwich." He braced himself against the sink, turning his face to the floor. "All I did was make a fucking sandwich!"

Jacob rested one hand on his shoulder.

The cold leached through him, and he threw off his brother's arm. "Why aren't you angry?" he yelled. His eyes began to burn, and he pushed everything that made them burn into the black pit under his heart. "I'd be so goddamn angry."

Jacob smiled. "Even after this big bad thing, I get the only thing I ever wanted. You'll still be here when I'm gone."

The blackness consumed him. He picked up a glass on the counter and hurled it to the floor. Shards hit the baseboards and ricocheted like bumper cars. He wanted one of them to hit him, maybe even nick an artery. *Serve him right if I went first,* he thought. *Make him see what it's like.*

Jacob squatted and picked up the mail he'd swept onto the floor, dropping it on the table. "We got work to do. You going to help or not?"

Ezra sighed. He knew there'd be a day when he forgot what his brother looked like, when he'd give anything to be staring into Jacob's near-lashless blue eyes. But in that moment, seeing the placid acceptance on his brother's face, he wished he were in Timbuktu. "At least shake the glass out first, you dumbass."

He snatched the pile of mail and shook it over the floor, then resumed sorting. He tossed the car and health insurance bills back onto the floor. Then he pulled out a flyer printed on a glossy half-sheet. He scanned it once, then twice, wondering if he'd missed something. "This is it."

"What is?"

He held it up for Jacob to see.

His brother narrowed his eyes as he read the thick block type.

Come see the Sinners' Bible, the flyer said. You're invited to an informal Q&A session with Associate Librarian Avi Druckman. Our copy is one of only eleven in the world! See this priceless historical document and hear about its place in history from Professor Elizabeth Brandon. Join us in the Rare Book & Manuscript Room at Ford Library – 6 p.m. on March 15.

"I don't get it." Jacob frowned. "A book?"

"A priceless book." He shook his head. The only people who used that word were the ones with money. The rest of them knew everything had a price. "This is it. We can do this."

A university would be much easier to hit than a bank. Banks had security guards who carried guns. A handful of professors would never see it coming.

He glanced at the Farm Bureau calendar on the wall.

The presentation was a month and a half away. Plenty of time to plan.

The flyer showed a big gray building in the background, ugly and modern with tiny Lego windows that probably didn't open. Two people were in the foreground—a skinny white guy with glasses and an afro, and a smiling blonde who looked more like a movie star than a professor.

"She's hot," Jacob said, pointing at the blonde.

"Want to meet her?" he asked. "I think I can arrange it."

CHAPTER FOUR

*H*enrietta Maria, *Queen* of England, reached into the sooty grate to rescue the small book. Her fingertips slid through the soft pile of ash, closing around the spine. She shook it over the floor to remove most of the debris and looked over her shoulder.

Charles was gone.

She knew where to find him, but it would be best to leave him alone for a few moments. He'd stalk down the hall to his study and reach for his father's book, the *Basilikon Doron*. Whenever he felt unsure of himself, he sought the comfort of his father's words. James I had been a firm believer in the Divine Right of Kings. As long as Charles believed that, too, he could find the strength to do what he must. He hated punishing people. He hated conflict. But in this case, she would ensure his will held firm. Someone had made a terrible mistake, perhaps even committed a crime.

But that wasn't why she wanted this heretic Bible.

She wanted it because it was a sign from God.

He was reminding her of the many ways in which her family had failed Him.

She held it up and blew the last of the ash from the cover. It fell to the floor like snow. "Why must You punish me this way?" she whispered.

A punishment from God was the only explanation for the nightmare plaguing her sleep.

Every night, she saw a man dressed in green lying on a bed. His face was the color of an eel's belly, streaked with sweat and slime. Blood crusted his lips and chin. The assassin's knife had penetrated his torso, sliding easily between the second and third rib, and again between the fifth and sixth.

It was her father, Henri Quatre, the previous King of France. As she watched, an angel of the Lord appeared before him. Instead of embracing him and carrying him to eternal glory, the angel raised a sword of flame and struck off his head. The head fell to the floor and rolled toward her feet, long black hair trailing behind it. When it touched her, the eyes opened, weeping streams of blood.

The problem was that her father did not have long black hair.

Her husband, Charles, did.

She shivered and grasped at her furs. Even the memory of the dream made her cold. "Why must You punish me this way?" she said again.

Seven years ago, she had been sent from France to cement the alliance with England. But unlike most princesses, her mission was not simply to bear Charles Stuart's children. Her country had negotiated the right for her to remain a practicing Catholic, even as she married a prince sworn to defend the Anglican faith. The Holy Father himself had told her that her true mission was to rescue Charles from heresy. She was to convert him and, by extension, all of England back to the True Faith.

"I was fifteen," she whispered, sliding her fingers across the cover of the Bible. "How could You have asked such a thing of me?"

But age was no excuse.

Jeanne d'Arc had raised the siege of Orléans at eighteen.

God had sent her the dream as a warning. If she failed, Charles would be killed and it would all be her fault. She had to work faster.

But how?

Charles's court hated her.

They hated her confessor and her chapel. They hated her for refusing to be crowned as their queen in an Anglican sacrament. But how could she betray the Holy Father and the True Faith and participate in a heretic's ritual? She was a daughter of France, born of a king anointed by God.

But that thought was troublesome, too.

Her father had been baptized a Catholic. In his youth, he had turned from the True Faith to become a Huguenot, then turned again in order to win the crown. The great Henri IV, who joked that Paris was worth a Mass, had then spent his entire married life humiliating her mother as he strayed from the marriage bed. No French king had ever bedded the number of women her father had. Indeed, her father had broken every vow it was possible to break, divorcing his first wife, changing religions, and betraying her mother. It had all ended in a Parisian alley, when a madman named Ravaillac plunged a dagger between her father's ribs. She had been five months old, with no memory of him as king or father.

What was she supposed to think of him based on what he left behind? A trail of bastards, proof that he had violated the Seventh Commandment with no remorse whatsoever…yet he was the most beloved king in the nation's long history. Never had the French people wept as they had at his death.

She could not reconcile it in her mind.

How many times could one abjure a faith without attracting the wrath of God? How many times could one bend God's laws to satisfy one's own desires? Had God grown weary of her father's shifting loyalties? First Huguenot, now Catholic, first married to Margot, then Marie, first bedding the chambermaid and then the milkmaid, with a countess thrown in for sport.

God remembered such things.

Why else did the Bible say the Lord God will visit the iniquity of the fathers on the children, to the third and the fourth generation? If there were any truth to that verse, Henri IV's sins would be visited upon her, her children, and her children's children.

Or upon Charles, as her dream seemed to foretell.

And now this Bible appeared, with its horrible misprint, calling to her of one of her father's two great sins.

It was no mistake.

God did not make mistakes.

"You seek vengeance on my blood," she said. "To punish my father's sins."

She had to keep Charles close, both to her and to the True Faith. Converting him was the only way to release the curse her father had set upon them all with his wickedness. If she failed, the avenging angel with the sword would come for them all.

"No," she whispered to the angel. "You shall not have him."

She clutched the false Bible to her chest, a visible reminder of what she had to do, no matter the cost.

CHAPTER FIVE

"*They totally Photoshopped* you," Natalie Brandon said, eyeing her sister's faculty portrait. "Are you sure Crawford didn't tell you about this?"

"It's a punishment. He has the whole Religious Studies department to pull from, and I'm the one who gets the call." Beth crumpled the pink message slip, delivered to her faculty mailbox that morning. "He didn't even have the balls to tell me in person."

"Seriously." She held up the glossy flyer so Beth could see it. "No crows' feet, no laugh lines, nothing. Maybe you should thank him."

Beth snatched the flyer from her hand. "I'm only thirty-six, for Pete's sake."

"The freshmen in your Western Civ class were born in 1996."

"How did we get so goddamn old?"

"Speak for yourself." She pointed at the swear jar on her sister's desk.

Beth dug in her purse and shoved a dollar into the jar. "What do I know about the Bible? Nothing. What do I know about seventeenth-century printing customs? Nothing. What do I know about the struggle between Anglicans, Presbyterians, and Catholics in early modern England? Next to nothing. Who the fuck—" her hand dove into her purse—"would pick me for this?"

Would you like my help? Belial asked. *I know everything about the Bible.*

"No one asked you," she said.

"The Sinners' Bible." Beth shook her blonde bob. "It's only famous because of a mistake. That's what my career has come to—talking about typos."

"Where's the typo?"

Beth uncrumpled the chancellor's note. "Exodus 20:14. Like we're supposed to know it by heart or something."

"Don't look at me," she said. "I don't trust books without page numbers."

"All I remember about Exodus is Charlton Heston in *The Ten Commandments.*"

"He should have stayed with Anne Baxter."

"We're going to hell," Beth said.

Yes, Belial answered.

"No," she replied.

The angel flicked her with a wing and a white-hot streak of pain strobed behind her ear. She pressed her palms to the desk.

"Is it Belial?" Beth asked softly.

She nodded.

The angel, called Belial, crouched in the airless space above her brain, his wings folded over her parietal and frontal lobes. When they touched her, they lit up her skull like a pinball machine.

It had been that way since she was nine years old. She'd been in fourth grade, standing at the chalkboard in Mrs. Wilson's class. Suddenly, a searing pain had made her drop the chalk and press both palms to her head. She'd felt something moving beneath her skull, something with a human form and enormous feather-covered wings. She'd closed her eyes to shut out the blinding white light that accompanied the pain, but it only made the creature struggle harder to open its wings. When the creature realized her skull was the obstacle in its way, it spoke to her. "I have things I want to show you. But I have to open my wings to do it. Will you let me?"

Through the shock of fear and pain, she'd said yes.

Her body fell in a faint at the chalkboard. The next thing she knew, she was floating above it, with the creature at her side. All the pain and the noise and the light were gone. "My name is Belial," he said. "I live inside you now."

"Are you an angel?" she'd asked.

"Look around you and tell me what you think I am."

He waved his arm and she saw that they were no longer in a classroom. They were in a camp ringed with barbed wire. A man in black whipped a line of marching men, all emaciated, all wearing striped pajamas. A strange sort of snow fell from the sky, sticking to her hair and eyelashes. When the man with the whip turned to her, smiling a black and broken smile, she'd woken up in a hospital bed, screaming.

The doctors had all sorts of official-sounding explanations for what had happened. A sudden drop in blood pressure had resulted in a coma, the body's protective reaction to a pulse of just twenty-nine beats per minute. But they couldn't explain what had caused the drop in the first place, and they couldn't find Belial, no matter how many X-rays and CAT scans they did. He was there, though. She felt him. Every time he shifted his wings, the feathers pricked her brain like needles.

No one believed her when she told them that was why she was crying.

Instead, they prodded and poked her and locked her up in strange rooms, with bright lights strobing for hours on end. *We can't treat her,* they said to her parents, *until we can reproduce the seizure.*

She'd begged Belial to show himself, to do something to help her. He refused. *I belong with you now, little one,* he'd said. In the end, the doctors had shrugged their shoulders and let the psychiatrists argue among themselves. The state children's hospital had finally decided Belial was a hallucination, strong enough to induce physical effects because of her overdeveloped hypothalamus. They settled on a diagnosis of early-onset paranoid schizophrenia, and prescribed her a flood of mind-numbing medication.

The embarrassment of having a mentally ill daughter who needed constant care was too much for her mother to bear. She made friends with bottles of all shapes and sizes, rousing herself only to put Natalie's next pill in a spoonful of grape jelly. Her father worked in an office by day, and retreated into his study by night. Beth had been the one to feed her, wash her, dress her, and brush her hair. In return, she'd helped Beth with her homework, trying to remember not to do it in pink or purple ink.

Even before Belial, her brain could do things most others couldn't. When Beth stayed at school for track practice, she'd watch her sister's favorite shows and recite them word-for-word when Beth came home. She'd been able to tally grocery bills to the penny before she even knew what fabric softener was. After Belial, she could still do those things, but now she had his commentary to provide the context a nine-year-old lacked.

It had taken her a long time to realize he didn't always have her best interests at heart.

Beth was the only one she could trust.

Not Belial.

Never Belial.

He was the reason the other kids at school hated her. Before she'd learned to keep her mouth shut when he spoke to her, she'd answered him out loud. The other kids called her Nuthouse Natalie. After her second suspension for fighting, midway through fifth grade, her parents had pulled her out of school. Until the day they died and Beth moved home to take care of her, she'd barely left the house.

The three of them—she, Beth, and Belial—had developed a tense but stable working relationship. Beth believed in cognitive therapy, Belial believed in himself, and she believed in the welcoming numbness of whiskey and vodka. There were still times when Belial overwhelmed her, making her do things she didn't really want to do. She snaked her hand under the right sleeve of her sweatshirt and stroked the puffy silver scarflesh. She had one scar on each arm, a thin slit running from wrist to elbow. They itched when it was cold.

"And here's the best part," Beth continued. "Crawford will be at the presentation. Watching me. Judging me."

She opened her mouth to say it wasn't true, but it was.

Are you surprised he feels this way? Belial asked. *You lie to him on a daily basis.*

"He doesn't know that," she grumbled.

He knows you're lying about something. That's far worse.

They were lying about lots of things, actually.

Crawford didn't know about Belial, thanks to HIPAA regulations. All he knew was that she'd had health issues in the past, requiring Beth to act as her legal guardian. He didn't trust either of them, and made no secret of it. She'd have felt bad if he wasn't a dick. "I'll protect you from Crawford."

"You and what army?" Beth glanced at the message slip. "Looks like the book is already on campus. Avi has it in the rare book room."

It's cursed, you know, the angel said.

"So am I."

That whole family is cursed.

"What's he saying?" Beth asked.

"The Kennedys are cursed."

That's not the family I meant, little one.

"Honest mistake."

"What do the Kennedys have to do with this?" Beth asked.

"Nothing, apparently." A flicker of interest roused her attention. If not the Kennedys, who was Belial talking about? "Beth, when was the Sinners' Bible printed?"

Her sister glanced at the message slip. "1631."

Now do you know which family I mean?

She visualized the chronology of English kings, a series of portraits from a book she'd read in her father's library. The chronology stopped when she reached a man with long, dark hair and a melancholy face. "You're not serious."

Look what happened to him. To all of them. Are you saying you don't believe me?

"Not serious?" Beth asked. "Who's not serious?"

"The Joker."

"I thought Anne Baxter's episodes were with the Penguin."

"Egghead," she said absent-mindedly. Her heart beat faster as she ran through the chronology of rulers again, moving a few slots back and a few slots forward from the sad, long-haired man. "Beth, Belial's not talking about the Kennedys."

"Oh, good. Because looks, money, power, charisma, why should they have everything? Leave some curses for the rest of us, right?"

"If the Sinners' Bible was printed in 1631, it's the King James version. As in James Stuart, son of Mary Stuart and father of Charles Stuart."

Beth blinked. "No. Absolutely not."

"There's a Stuart curse," she breathed. "An honest-to-God curse."

"We don't know that."

"Belial was right about the Romanov letters. Why couldn't he be right about this?"

"Those were letters. Actual physical things that could be found."

"So is this book. What if it has something to do with the Stuart curse?"

"The Stuart curse was venereal disease. Besides, Mary, Queen of Scots was beheaded in 1587, way before the Sinners' Bible was printed. The timeline is off."

Belial shuffled his wings, careful to keep the edges from touching her skull. *Did the Bible curse the family? Or did the family curse the Bible? Do you even know how a curse is cast?*

"He says it's real," she said. "And he's going to teach us how to curse people."

That is not what I said.

"I can't deal with this right now." Beth sank into her desk chair and massaged both temples with her index fingers. Her teeth scraped a piece of dry skin on her lip. "I have an op-ed on the new Russian imperialism due at the *New York Times* in a week, a book proposal due in four, and I'm still trying to wrangle that RFP from the National Endowment for the Arts. Then, last night, Seth asked me for help with advanced algebra." Her sister looked up, tears gleaming in her eyes. "I'm a bad mother, Nat."

"I've never seen a better mother," she said softly. "Not in the whole world."

"What the hell is a polynomial?" Beth wailed. "I can't help my own kid because I don't have time to re-learn math and I feel like shit about it."

"Let me help."

"You know I hate asking you for things."

"You can ask, Beth." Her scars started to tingle and she scratched the right one with a jagged fingernail. "You're the only one who can."

"That's not the impression I got in London."

She closed her eyes. *Constantine.* He believed in her, she knew that much. But he had his own problems, and they were occupying most of his time. "He's not here. You are."

"And I always will be. I love you, sis."

"Then bring Seth over and we'll kick the shit out of some polynomials." This time, she scratched the scar on her left arm.

I can feel it when you do that, Belial said. *I don't like it.*

Beth sighed. "So I'm really doing this, then…a talk on the Sinners' Bible."

"Let me help with that, too. What kind of background info do you need me to dig up?"

"It's been so long since I studied pre-industrial England." Beth shrugged out of her black blazer and hung it on the coat rack next to her desk. "Charles Stuart was the only English king to be condemned to death in a court of law by his own people. What are the odds?"

"One point six percent. If you start with the House of Wessex, and count William and Mary as one."

"Poor Charles."

"Beth, what if there really is a Stuart curse?"

I told you, Belial said.

"Belial says—"

"I know what bastard says." Beth picked up the crumpled pink message slip and aimed a jump shot, bouncing it off the rim of the trash can.

Natalie smiled. She couldn't help it. Her perfect sister, the one with the perfect job and the perfect house and the perfect wardrobe, couldn't shoot a basket to save her life. "The Warriors called. The Heisman's yours."

Beth grinned. "I always wanted to play in the World Series."

"You could bring Crawford one of those big foam fingers."

"He'd just use it to point at me during staff meetings." Beth sighed. "Seriously, Nat, whatever you do, don't mention a curse in front of Crawford. I don't think he has a sense of humor about these things."

He'll need one, Belial said.

She shivered and dug her nails into her scar. "No curse," she said. "I promise."

CHAPTER SIX

The Bible lay in a trunk under her cerulean gown, where she'd packed it for the journey from the Palais Royal. She didn't dare leave it behind. That book was a reminder of all the ways she'd failed Charles, her children, the Holy Father, and the True Faith. Were there Stuart blood spattered upon its pages, it could not torment her more.

Henrietta Maria clutched at her stomach.

Twelve years, six months, and fourteen days later, she still dreamed of Charles's death. But her dream had been wrong, as it turned out. The angel of death had come wielding an axe, not a sword.

And she was the reason that axe had fallen.

That was what they said, anyway, in England and here in France.

The English civil war? All the fault of that Papist queen, who kept Charles from supporting the Calvinists on the Continent. That Papist queen, who urged him to dissolve Parliament and rule with nothing but the Divine Right bestowed on him by God. That Papist queen, who told him to arrest the only men in Parliament trying to save the country. In the end, the Parliamentarians had won. Her Charles had gone to his death wearing two shirts to keep from shivering in the January cold. He hadn't wanted the people to think he was afraid to die.

Did I really do all those things? she wondered. *Or did I simply believe in him and urge him to do what he felt was right?*

She felt sick every time she thought it was the former.

Why would God have marked her out for such misery? Were her father's sins so great that they must be visited upon her and her children, as she had believed when she was younger? Henri IV was still the most beloved king in French history. How could someone so loved be so far from God's favor? Did that mean her beloved Charles, who had been most unloved, was in God's favor?

"I don't understand what You want from me," she whispered, turning toward the window.

Her room overlooked the gardens. A shaft of sunlight streamed through the glass, illuminated the battered corners of her trunk at the foot of the bed.

God had warned her twice—once with the misprinted Bible, and again with her nightmare. Still she had failed. Charles was dead, England remained Anglican, and she was a pauper, living entirely on the charity of her sister-in-law, Anne of Austria, mother of the French king Louis XIV.

Through the loss of her home, her crown, her husband, and six of her children, that book had remained, a witness and a companion to her grief. So here it was, tormenting her still as she accompanied her daughter, Henriette, on this parody of a honeymoon.

The wedding had been uneventful, save for Henriette's tear-stained cheeks and the smile on Anne of Austria's lips. That smile would fade when Anne learned the truth. She had deemed Henriette too poor a prospect for her beloved son. As if a granddaughter of Henri IV were not fit to become Queen of France! Anne had ushered her boy king into the arms of a cold Spanish princess instead. But Anne would learn that both of her precious sons had broken God's vows.

Oh yes, she thought, looking down into the gardens. *Even her precious Louis.*

She leaned forward and pressed her hands to the glass. The gardens were lined with hedgerows as tall as a man—purposefully so, arranged in a maze. Henriette stood at the entrance in a gown of pale yellow, her shoulders bare to the summer sun.

"Cover up, child," she muttered.

But in her heart, that wasn't what she wanted her daughter to do.

Because her married daughter was reaching for the hand of a man who was not her husband. That husband was in the stables with the Chevalier de Lorraine, occupied with acts and thoughts that the tribes of Israel had forbidden in Leviticus. Instead, Henriette's tiny hand slid into the grasp of her husband's brother, Louis, the fourteenth king of that name.

The man she loved.

The man she should have married, were it not for Anne of Austria's meddling.

I am the wickedest mother ever, she thought. *But I want her to have him.* Henriette deserved some little happiness, and Anne of Austria deserved to reap what she had sown and watch her son covet his brother's wife in full view of his court.

Louis brought Henriette's hand to his lips. She dropped in a curtsy, her quick breath pushing her breasts above her tightly corseted bodice.

Henrietta Maria watched his dark eyes devour her daughter. He slid one hand up her arm, twining his fingers in her black hair, pulling her lips to his for a kiss. When their lips touched, he clasped her to him.

She recognized the look.

He was a king in love.

She sighed and leaned her head against the window frame. Another French king was straying from the marriage bed. Did that mean Louis, too, would be assassinated? Or would God's vengeance strike the object of the king's desire instead?

"No," she pleaded. "If You must take one of us, take me in her place."

Louis pulled Henriette around the corner of a hedgerow, into the maze. One hand was already beneath her skirt. Henrietta Maria wiped a tear from her cheek. What sort of mother cried tears of happiness to see her daughter dishonored?

"I am cursed," she said. "And so are you, my love."

She turned to her trunk and dug the Bible out from under her folded gown. *Let it be a record of my failure*, she thought, *since it must have been I who brought this curse upon our family.* She carried it to the bureau, where a quill and ink pot sat ready for her. Most families recorded their births and deaths in the front of their Bibles, a proud history of ownership and achievement.

"Let our backward history be written here," she said, turning to the inside back cover.

She picked up the quill, dipped it in the ink, and said a prayer for those consumed by the strange curse that ran in her family's blood. It brought adultery and dethronement and execution, each repudiating a holy sacrament—marriage, anointing, and baptism.

She sobbed as she wrote.

"My father."

Henri.

"My husband."

Charles.

Her hand hesitated beneath her husband's name. Would her daughter's be written there in time?

"Please," she prayed. "Let me write no more names."

CHAPTER SEVEN

Ezra pulled the Chevy into the university's faculty parking lot and looked at the dozen streetlights surrounding it. Every other post had a callbox with a flashing blue light.

Jacob pointed. "What are those things?"

Ezra slapped his hand. "Don't point. Don't talk. Don't do anything to make them look."

"I want to know what they are."

"They're for girls."

"But they're blue."

"They're so girls can call the police if someone attacks them."

"Is that what they do here?" Jacob asked, craning his neck to look at the library, a six-floor structure in ugly gray cement.

"That and give parking tickets." He glanced at his watch. It had taken twenty-two minutes to get here from the freeway. Next time, they wouldn't have twenty-two minutes. On the night of the robbery, the truck would have to be left behind. Maybe he could steal a Mustang and leave it in this lot beforehand.

Jacob liked Mustangs.

He turned to look at his brother.

Black grease rimmed Jacob's fingernails. His blue flannel looked like a map of Micronesia, dotted with burn holes from welding spatter. For this to work, at least one of them had to pass for a student. Would anyone believe Jacob was a football player?

"Hey," he said. "Who's better at the long pass, Stabler or Plunkett?"

Jacob drummed his fingers against his leg. "Pulled the blower motor earlier today. Everything looked fine. Maybe it's one of the blend door actuators."

"And there's my answer."

He rolled down his window and glanced in the rearview mirror. It was a long shot, but he might be able to pass for a student if he'd changed his major a few times and been held back because he couldn't get the classes he needed. A group of girls walked by, all wearing sweatshirts with the blue and white Rosemont crest. He couldn't afford to buy one, and he couldn't risk stealing one—the student store was probably full of cameras, just waiting to pick off shoplifters. He'd have to improvise.

"They have police here?" Jacob asked.

"A campus cop shop."

"They carry guns?"

"That's what we're here to find out."

Jacob picked up a switchblade from the truck's door pocket.

"Put that down," he said.

Jacob flicked it open, but kept it in his lap. "I got a bad feeling about this."

"I can handle it."

"Maybe I don't want you to."

"You don't know what you want."

"Ezra."

"What?"

"Look at me."

He turned his head and saw the tip of the knife sunk a quarter-inch into Jacob's index finger. "I can't feel it," his brother said.

"Goddamn it, Jacob." His eyes flew from mirror to mirror, hoping no one was watching.

"Fell while I was putting my boots on this morning, too. Isn't that how the doc said it would happen?"

"You'll get your balance back once they cut out the tumor."

"I don't want to do this."

"Put that away before you get us in trouble. Where'd you even get that thing?"

"Texarkana." His brother pulled the tip of the knife out of his finger. "It's not like I haven't seen anything, Ezra. I've been places."

"Not enough."

"I don't want to do this."

"We still need to eat, don't we?"

"Who's going to buy a book?"

"I'll find someone."

"Who?"

"Not your problem."

"Who?" Jacob said, leaning toward him.

"Excuse me," said a high-pitched voice. "Do we have a problem here?" A grey-haired man in a security uniform walked up to his window and put his hands on his hips, craning his neck to see inside the truck.

"No, sir," he said. In his peripheral vision, he saw Jacob drop the switchblade back into the door's side pocket.

"You can't park here," the old man said. "You're blocking the exit."

Ezra glanced at the man's utility belt. He had a walkie-talkie and a flashlight, no gun. He flashed the guy a friendly smile. "I'm picking up a friend at the library. This is the library, isn't it?"

The old man nodded. "Student parking is on the other side of the quad."

"Could have sworn the map said it was right here. I'll show you." He fumbled with the pile of napkins on the bench seat.

"You don't need a map to read the signs." The old guy pointed at the row of signs, one posted in front of each parking space: FACULTY ONLY. "Move along now," he said, circling his arm like a traffic cop.

"What time does the library close tonight? Maybe I got the time wrong."

"Nine o'clock."

Wrong, he thought. According to their website, the library closed at 11 p.m., and the 24-hour reading room never closed. So much for an organized and efficient first responder. "You've been a big help," he said, nodding at the man. "Have a nice day."

The old man nodded back and adjusted his blue cap.

He put the truck in gear and pulled out of the lot. "It's a good day, brother. What did that magic 8-ball used to say when we were kids?"

"Concentrate and ask again."

"Outlook good," he said. "That's the one I remember."

The truck slowed to a crawl as he waited for a pair of students on bikes to make a turn. Jacob reached for the climate control and turned the dial all the way to the right. "It's cold."

A thumping sound clacked behind the glove box.

"Vacuum connection," Jacob said, frowning. "Maybe it's leaking."

"I thought you said it was the actuator something or other."

"I don't know what it is. All I know is it takes money to fix."

He sighed. "One more month," he said. "Just hang on one more month."

CHAPTER EIGHT

Her hands were cold. Not five minutes after the last breath left her body, Henriette's hands felt like the frozen skin on the Grand Canal in winter. Philippe, duc d'Orléans, curled his long fingers around her palm. He couldn't bear to look at her face.

"Je suis désolé," he whispered. "You know everything now."

A warm hand fell on his shoulder and he shook it off. His brother, the king, could go anywhere he pleased, even places he was not wanted. "Get out," Philippe growled.

"Brother, you're upset," Louis said. "Let me—"

"Get out!" he roared. "For one moment, let me be alone with her."

Louis's dark eyes narrowed. "So you can pretend you were a good husband to her? So you can pretend you loved her?" The king shook his head. "You never loved her."

"I did," he said. "In my own way."

"Your way would have killed her years ago," Louis hissed. "She would have been dead of a broken heart instead of…" The king stopped.

Philippe knew what he was thinking.

Henriette was twenty-six. There was no good reason for her to have fallen, shrieking in agony, onto the kitchen floor. Especially not a mere thirty days after delivering the requirements of Louis's secret treaty to her brother in England—a treaty that required King Charles II, defender of the Anglican faith, to convert to Catholicism.

That was pure Louis, playing God even among his fellow sovereigns.

Philippe turned away from his brother, back to the body on the bed. Henriette's cheeks were hollow, her color vanished. She was made of wax. She might wake at any minute and look upon him with those eyes, the dark sloe eyes of her mother. "Find out who has done this," he said. "Since you are the one who killed her."

He heard the rustle of stiff brocade as Louis straightened. "I did no such thing. I asked something of her, and she granted it to me."

"It was dangerous and you knew it."

"She did it out of love for me."

"As you knew she would! You used her, brother, far more unkindly than ever I did."

"I did not cause her death. I swear it."

"Then that family is cursed!" Philippe cried. "There is no other explanation for it. Her father, her grandfather, her great-grandmother…something terrible floods their veins. My poor daughters, how I fear for them!"

"They have our blood, too," Louis said. "They will escape. I swear it."

"Go," Philippe said. "Now."

"You cannot—"

Philippe rose to his feet. "If you do not leave this room, so help me, I will beat you into the floor the way I did when we were under our mother's skirts. Let us see whose blood is anointed and whose is not when they are mingled on the floor together. Can you tell the difference, brother?"

Louis blinked. His gaze flickered over Philippe's shoulder, to Henriette's purpled face and lips. "You are beside yourself with grief. At any other time, brother, that statement would amount to treason."

I don't care, Philippe thought, turning his back and kneeling beside the bed. It had been wrong of Louis to send a sister-in-law on a mission more suited to diplomats and spies. His brother had always cared more for glory than for the women he welcomed into his bed.

He waited for the echoes of Louis's footsteps to die.

"Whose betrayal cut you deeper?" he asked. Was it his own, conducted with the Chevalier de Lorraine, or Louis's, using her for political gain at the potential cost of her life? "I loved you as best I could."

He reached once more for Henriette's cold hand. They had been lovers, as required of a man and wife joined in the sacrament of marriage. She had given him two pretty daughters, whose tiny flailing hands made him happier than he had imagined a child ever could. But their hearts belonged to others—hers to his brother, and his to the Chevalier. If anyone was to blame, it was his mother, who had forbidden Louis to marry Henriette, the penniless daughter of a murdered king.

"Would you have been happy?" he asked. "With my brother?"

He waited for Henriette's ghost to answer, but it never happened. She would not speak to him. Perhaps she could not. They had broken commandments, all three of them—coveting a brother's wife, adultery, sodomy. If God were real, and if He had watched them lie and steal and hurt each other, perhaps they were all bound for hell.

His gaze fell on the table beside her bed. A small Bible lay next to a pitcher of water and a handkerchief stained with gore so dark it looked like tar. "You have no need of this now," he said, reaching for the Bible.

His fingers itched to throw it into the fire.

God's word was the source of all misery for those like him.

A red ribbon marked a page near the beginning. He let the book fall open in his hand, wondering which passage Henriette had chosen to read as she'd choked on her own blood and foaming bile. The pages were thin and brown, with a red line marking the left-hand margin of the verses. The type had bled and faded over time.

Like we all have, he thought.

His English was not good, but the words on that particular page were simple enough for him to translate. She had marked the page with the Ten Commandments. His eye fell upon a particular verse:

12 Honour thy father and thy mother, that thy dayes may bee long vpon the land which the lord thy God giveth thee.

Philippe curled his lip.

His father's death had turned his brother into a king, into a consecrated god among men who never let him forget his own inferiority.

His mother had done everything possible to make him see he was nothing in comparison to her beloved Louis. Dressing him in skirts, calling him her little girl, anything to keep him from realizing who he was and what he might be—the king, if Louis were to die. She would have sacrificed his life in a heartbeat if it ensured the safety of her firstborn. He could love her, but he could not honor her.

He forced his eyes down the page.

13 Thou fhalt not kill.

His brother, the god-king, had sent him into battle where he had lost count of the number of Spaniards he killed. Did it still count, he wondered, when those deaths had been required for the glory of a king? Would God remember that when it was his time to be judged?

He looked to the next commandment.

14 Thou fhalt commit adultery.

Jesus Christ almighty, he thought. What sort of God did those Anglicans pray to? No wonder Henriette had kept this with her, despite remaining a Catholic. It was the only Bible on the face of the Earth that would tell her to give into her heart's desire, leading her straight to his brother's bed.

He closed the Bible, leaving the red ribbon where it lay.

He wanted no part of it, of her, of his brother, of himself.

The only comfort he could imagine was in the arms of the Chevalier. But first, he would send this abomination of a book back to that cursed family. Let it leave France's shore and return to the heretics who had broken from the True Faith. Let it be on their heads whatever happened next.

CHAPTER NINE

*N*atalie *stared at* the deck of index cards she'd written for Beth's presentation that evening. Crawford had given Beth a 20-minute slot, which was nowhere near enough time to explain how things had gotten so fucked up in England in the 17th century.

I can sum it up, Belial said. *Three little words.*

"Bad hair day?"

The Roundheads discouraged all forms of personal vanity.

"They discouraged Charles I's head from being attached to his shoulders. Whatever happened to 'Thou shalt not kill'?"

You tell me, little one, Belial said. Suddenly, the scars on her arms began to itch.

"That was your fault and you know it."

At least the Roundheads took responsibility for their actions.

"Take responsibility for this." She reached for a pair of sharp black scissors on Beth's desk.

Would you rather I changed the subject?

"More than anything."

Shall we talk about the Stuart curse? This book is part of it.

"I don't care."

A curse is a living thing. Like a virus searching for a host.

"You would know."

I gave you time, and you refused to listen. We cannot wait any longer.

"I promised Beth. No curse."

The angel flicked her with a wing and pain sizzled across her skull. *I'm trying to protect you.*

"Could have fooled me." She narrowed her eyes in a squint, looking for her army-green messenger bag. She spotted it hanging on Beth's coat rack. Inside the bag was a bottle of vodka.

There are things no one knows about this book. If your sister revealed them, the world would listen. Crawford would listen. Isn't that what you want for her?

"Not like this."

She got up slowly and reached for her bag. A flash of memory lit up the blackness behind her eyes—a man with white hair, holding up a tarnished brass key. She had already discovered something that would make Beth untouchable, something far beyond Crawford's pay grade. But they were sworn to secrecy, for their own safety if nothing else.

Why won't you let me give you what you want?

"Because I promised Beth."

What if she never has this opportunity again?

"Maybe it's not the opportunity that's the problem. Maybe it's me." Beth had applied for the position of dean twice already. Crawford ignored her both times, even though she was the most qualified candidate.

Perhaps it is, little one.

"What have I ever done to Crawford? Why would he punish Beth because of me?"

You frighten him. You frighten everyone.

"I don't mean to."

It is the way God created you.

"Then change it," she whispered, crushing the bag to her chest. "Change me into someone better."

But I love you as you are.

"I want to be someone better! Why can't you do that for me?"

We don't have time for this, the angel said. *We must talk about—*

"No." She heaved the bag strap over her head. "I'm tired of being someone's problem."

You'll be sorry, the angel said.

She thought of everything Beth had sacrificed to help her. The hours of behavioral therapy, the cooking, the cleaning, the crying…and she did it all even though there was no happy ending for them. Belial couldn't be stopped. He would always be there inside her, waiting to destroy what she loved most. "I already am."

She ran out of Beth's office, down the hall to the bathroom. If she drank herself into a stupor, it had to be there, not in Beth's office. She could at least keep Crawford from having one more reason to hate her.

She pushed open the bathroom door and perched on the toilet in an empty stall. Her fingers unlatched the flap of her bag and dug inside for the familiar plastic shape. Belial sighed when the first gulp of vodka hit her throat.

Not too much, he said. *Please.*

"Suck ethanol," she said, raising the bottle once more.

§

Three hours later

NATALIE UNLOCKED BETH'S office door and stumbled through it, flinging out her right hand to flip the light switches. Something pink on the floor caught her eye and she bent over.

It was a message slip, folded in half, with the initials B.B. jotted on top.

She picked it up and took it to her desk. It was smaller than Beth's, with none of the framed diplomas behind it. The only decoration she had was a framed photo of herself and Beth as girls. Beth smiled and pointed at the enormous gap where her two front teeth used to be. She looked like a ghost, thanks to her pale blue eyes. They had had never photographed well — too light, without enough contrast next to her skin.

She sank slowly into her chair, testing her vision.

Nothing was spinning. Things were still a little blurry, though, as if she were nearsighted.

She unfolded the message slip and blinked, turning it upside down and holding it at arm's length. There was no doubt as to the sender. Across the top, a row of bold black letters proclaimed FROM THE DESK of CHANCELLOR CRAWFORD.

Half an hour later, she had realized two things: Crawford definitely hated her, and he also wrote all his personal memos in cuneiform with his toes. Drunk or not, the man's handwriting was the worst she'd ever seen.

There was only one appropriate response, both to the indecipherable message and its contents. She folded the slip of paper in half, then used her fingernail to score the back corners into a diagonal. A few more creases, and the message slip's black headline had disappeared.

She picked up the paper airplane and aimed it at the trash can across the room. The plane undershot the target, nose-diving into the floor.

Mayday, Belial muttered.

She glanced at the clock. Three hours and five minutes—that's how much oblivion eight gulps of vodka had bought her. "Go away," she said. "You ruin everything."

It's coming, the angel said.

"I don't care."

Beth was due back from her lecture any minute. They were supposed to go through her notes for the Sinners' Bible talk, then walk over to the rare book room together. Beth's nerves still took hold of her every time she spoke in public. She needed to be in the venue as early as possible to calm herself down and find every available restroom. Although she didn't throw up before student lectures anymore, Professor Elizabeth Brandon still hurled every time she presented before her peers.

Beth was the best in the world at doing what scared her most.

And all I do is bring her down, she thought, glaring at the pink paper airplane beside the trash can. She reached into her pocket and fumbled for a familiar silver square.

I wouldn't do that if I were you, Belial said.

"You're not me."

Oh, but I am, little one.

She flicked the lighter into life. A yellow-orange flame swayed like a belly dancer, and she held it next to her hand.

Your sister is nervous enough. You won't help her by filling her office with the scent of burning flesh.

She moved the lighter closer to her head.

Or hair.

"Fine." She slid to the floor and crawled to the paper airplane. One flick of the lighter, and a topaz flame lit up the airplane's tail. "No more parachutes," she said, turning the plane nose-down.

Suddenly, she heard the clacking of Beth's heels in the hallway. The staccato thump of expensive Italian leather was accompanied by a baritone voice she recognized with a wave of nausea. "Son of a bitch," she said, waving the burning paper in the air. "What the hell is Crawford doing here?"

Talking about you, Belial said.

She blew out the flame, dropped the burned plane on Beth's desk, and lunged for the door of the adjoining conference room. She stumbled over the laces of her boots, but got the door shut a split second before Beth slid her key into the lock.

Her breath fogged the frosted window in the conference room door. She sank to her knees and held onto the doorknob for support. Through the blurred glass, she could see her sister's vibrant colors—bright blue suit, red blouse, platinum blond hair. Beth opened the door and stood aside, as if she were a stewardess.

Crawford followed. The silver rims of his glasses stood out against his black skin, echoing the burst of gray at his temples. He walked with his hands folded behind his back. *Only assholes and supervillains walk with their hands folded behind their back*, she thought.

Crawford sniffed the air. "Have you been smoking in here, Ms. Brandon? That's a direct violation of both state and university policy."

"I don't—" Then Beth's gaze landed on the charred paper airplane, a wisp of smoke curling above its tail. She flung out her arms and braced them against the desk to hide it. "What did you want to talk to me about, sir?"

"I thought my message made that obvious."

"I was hoping you could clarify the…um…action item."

"It's your research assistant."

"You mean my sister."

"In the capacity for which I pay her, she is your research assistant."

"Sir?"

"She was seen drinking in the women's bathroom, Ms. Brandon. A student called the medical center to report her. I believe the words 'more than Sigma Alpha Epsilon' were used."

Natalie hung her head. *I'm sorry*, she mouthed.

"I'll talk to her, sir," Beth said. "It won't happen again."

"I take my job seriously, Ms. Brandon. One of my responsibilities is providing role models for our students. If a member of our staff can't live up to that expectation, I have no choice but to fire them."

"I said it won't happen again."

Beth, stop, she thought. *You'll only make it worse.*

"If she causes a disruption again, she'll be fired without a reference, referred to campus police, and you will take an unpaid leave of absence. My university is not a charity."

"I agree completely," Beth said. "I couldn't have put the Sinners' Bible presentation together on such short notice without her. Natalie is the best research assistant I've ever had."

"Then she'd better earn her keep." Crawford tapped his watch. "Your presentation starts in an hour. I'd better see just how useful she's been to you, or there will be consequences, Ms. Brandon."

"Y—yes, sir." Her sister waited until Crawford's shoes had squeaked halfway down the hall. Then she shut the door and pressed both hands against it, as if she were holding the door of the Ark against the flood.

"Beth," she said softly, opening the conference room door.

Her sister spun, blue eyes wide, hand pressed to her chest. "Jesus, Nat, don't scare me like that."

"I'm sorry." She stepped into the office and closed the door behind her. "For everything."

"You have to be more careful. What were you thinking?"

"I thought I could handle it, but Belial wouldn't shut up. He said it's coming for us."

It is, the angel said.

"What is?"

"The Stuart curse."

"The Sinners' Bible has nothing to do with the Stuart curse. It's a book with a typo, nothing more."

"I know that. The vodka knows, too. It's only Belial who doesn't."

"Why were you drinking in the bathroom?"

"I didn't disturb anyone, I promise."

"I know, babe," Beth sighed.

"I can't stand feeling like I'm holding you back. Like Crawford hates you because of me."

"You're not holding me back. Remember that whole polynomial thing? Sometimes I need you just to function." Her sister shrugged. "If Crawford doesn't see that, he's an asshole."

"Belial said that if you talk about the curse, Crawford will listen."

"He won't. He cancelled Rodriguez's class on heresy and witchcraft in medieval Europe after it had full enrollment and fifty names on the wait list. I'm giving the talk exactly as you wrote it. I trust you a hell of a lot more than I trust Belial."

The angel sniffed. *All these years, and your sister still hates me.*

"I hate you, too."

The angel tapped her with the edge of a wing. A spear of

lightning zapped the right side of her skull.

Her eyes filled with tears of anger.

"Come here," Beth said, wrapping her arms around her. She leaned into Beth's chest and breathed in her sister's perfume—light, airy, with a hint of vanilla. Beth rocked in place and smoothed her hair. "We'll be fine. We always have."

"I'm sorry for the way I am."

"Hush," Beth said, pressing a kiss to her forehead.

No one understands you, the angel said. *As long as your sister stands by your side, they will believe of her what they do of you.*

I know, she thought.

They'll hate her and fear her, just like they do you.

I know, she thought.

A minute later, Beth let her go. She dredged her index finger under her eyes and smoothed her hair. "Crawford has both of us on a short leash tonight. Let's start walking to the library. I might need to hurl before Avi's talk."

"Might? You're like the Old Faithful of puke."

"Nat." A shadow darkened Beth's eyes. "Are you absolutely sure can you keep Belial under control for the next two hours? You can't drink in front of Crawford, not now."

"I'm sure," she said. "Get your notes. Let's go."

She waited until Beth turned her back, then grabbed the scissors on the desk and shoved them into her bag. *You will leave us alone tonight,* she told Belial. *Do this for her, or I swear, I'll stab myself in the heart just to shut you up.*

Be careful what you wish for, the angel said, folding his wings and bowing his head.

CHAPTER TEN

he courtiers were whispering. He wondered what had set them off this time. Had they placed bets on the hour of his death? Or were those Whig bastards plotting again? He hoped it was the former. He would tell Killigrew to place a bet for him on 4 a.m. That's how he wanted to go down in history—Charles II, the sovereign who won the betting pool for his own time of death.

If he won, he would instruct Killigrew to give the money to the queen.

That poor woman, he thought.

He wished it had been possible to love others without casting the specter of dishonor on her. Every time he told himself to stop, he found that he could not—not after the horrors of civil war, when Cromwell's men had hunted him like game. *If I survive*, he had told himself in those dark moments. *If I survive, I will never take this life for granted. I will be grateful for every warm bed and willing woman and every moment I am given to enjoy them both.*

It was not something he could make poor Catherine understand, nor was it something he could give up. For him, it was the meaning of being alive. But she, a good Catholic, always forgave him. She found a different meaning in being alive.

Before his mother had died, she told him that her father's adultery and multiple conversions had cursed their family. If that were true, what he was about to do would only anger God further. "Do not blame them," he whispered, thinking of the ones he left behind—his brother and two plump nieces. "Have mercy on us all."

But God had shown precious little mercy to the Stuarts so far.

His great-grandmother, Mary of Scots, had been beheaded by her cousin.

His grandfather, James I, had written pious treatises on demonology and witchcraft, and still the Catholics had tried to blow him up.

His own father had been beheaded by that monster Cromwell.

They said his beloved sister had been poisoned.

It appeared that he had fallen victim, now, too. After twenty-three years of marriage, he had sired at least twelve bastards…and no legitimate offspring to inherit his throne. He had failed in one of the primary duties of a king. His brother, Dull Jimmy, would become James II, King of England, Scotland, and Ireland.

He moved his left hand. James, standing at his bedside, knelt beside him. He thought about warning him, making sure his brother understood the curse that flowed in their veins. But if James was daft enough to remain oblivious, let him deal with the consequences. He could not summon the breath to enlighten him. "Be well to Portsmouth," he said, "and let not poor Nelly starve."

James's dark eyes glittered. "Only for love of you, dear brother."

"Send them away now," he said. "It is time."

James nodded. "Gentlemen," he said, turning to the small crowd ringed around his bedside. "The King wishes everybody to retire."

He closed his eyes and listened to the sounds of more whispers as the throng dispersed. Without them, he felt lighter.

A small door opened across the room. Through this narrow arch stepped John Huddleston, the priest who had helped him escape from his father's murderers thirty-three years before. He wished he had the breath to congratulate Huddleston on his foresight.

Huddleston hurried to his bedside and knelt. "Your Majesty, do you wish to be received into the Roman Catholic faith?"

"He does," James said.

"I do," he whispered.

Huddleston smiled a beatific smile that made him sure of his choice. The country wanted a Protestant king, and he had given them one. Now, in the hour of his death, let the country give God a Catholic king. If God cursed his family for their vacillation in their faith, there was no help for it now. He had made a promise to his sister, Henriette, all those years ago in Dover, when Louis XIV had sent her to negotiate with him in secret.

Promise me, Charles, she had said. *I could not bear the thought of you in hell. I have had to bear so much, but I would let it fall upon my shoulders willingly, if I knew that you were assured a place in Heaven.* She had reached up to his face, stroking his cheek with her tiny fingers. *You are the only man who never hurt me. Be that man in life and in death.*

She was the only woman who had never wanted anything from him.

Castlemaine and Kéroualle and Villiers, he loved them, yes, but they wanted his favors, his time, his kingly beneficence. From the day she was born, Minette had only wanted him. Now, she would greet him at the gate of Heaven, smiling and reaching for him with both hands.

"All right, Minette," he whispered, turning his head into the pillow as Huddleston made the sign of the cross over his body. "It is done."

CHAPTER ELEVEN

The taxi pulled up next to the student union. Ezra thrust a $20 bill at the cabbie and slung his backpack over his shoulder. The cuffs of his stolen blue sweatshirt barely reached his wrists. He forced himself not to yank on them again.

Jacob got out of the cab and stared at the four-story building, a gleaming glass-front structure with its name emblazoned in silver letters: THE JAMES SIMONS MEMORIAL STUDENT UNION. "How much money you think that guy had?"

"All of it." The sleeves of his sweatshirt crept up his forearm and he shoved his hands in his pockets to keep from tugging at them. "Stop staring. We're students, remember?"

A skateboarder rode by, flipping his board as he jumped three steps to the grassy quad between the student union and the library. There were paved walkways all around the quad, but the kid held his board and walked across the grass.

He fell in behind the kid. At least one of them would look like they belonged.

Jacob's long legs kept up with fewer strides as they cut a path through the grass. From the corner of his eye, he saw his brother gawk at the six-story library looming at the other end of the quad. "I told you not to stare. It's just a library."

"It looks like the Death Star."

"So it's the Death Star. Who cares? I'm Han Solo and you're Chewbacca. We make it out of this just fine."

"What about the sequels?"

"We renegotiate our contracts for script approval."

Ezra waited for Jacob's smile, but it didn't happen. A tendril of fear wound its way around his heart. Something had changed over the past few weeks. Jacob moved slower, ate less, and tired easily, but he didn't have the memory problems the doctor had warned them about. *There's still time*, he thought. *There has to be.*

"You could have made it in a place like this, you know," Jacob said.

"Yeah." He glared at the neck tat on kid in front of him. "I fit right in with the guys in Sigma Phi Asshole."

"I wish you'd—"

"Stop," he said. "Just stop. I need to concentrate."

But he didn't. He'd already planned everything, from the minute he'd pull his gun to the route they'd take to reach the getaway car. It was stashed behind the grad student housing unit, where older students wouldn't look out of place. There were two sets of license plates in his backpack, courtesy of the U.S. Postal Service. *This is what I do*, he thought, looking sideways at Jacob. *Everything else is just a fairy tale.*

But his brother wouldn't believe it no matter how many times he said it, so he crossed the quad in silence.

A walking path separated the library from a sandy rectangle, where hundreds of bikes rested their tires in hollow concrete blocks. Some were rusted out, with flat tires or bent wheel frames. He shook his head. There was something wrong with a kid who'd pay tens of thousands of dollars for a degree, but couldn't learn to change a tire.

He looked at his watch.

5:57 p.m.

"Come on," he said. "It's time."

They crossed the walking path and the concrete pavilion that led to the library's entrance. He pushed through the revolving door and glanced over his shoulder.

Jacob stood outside, staring at the door.

"Come on," he muttered.

What if Jacob got a headache? Or lost his balance and fell? Or…

No, he thought. *Not that. Not yet.*

He gripped the straps of his backpack. Finally, his brother shook his head and pushed through the revolving door. "What the hell was that about?" he hissed, once Jacob had caught up.

Jacob smiled. "Never thought I'd go through a revolving door again. You remember the one at the bank, when Mom used to take us?"

"She left me in the car."

"I always brought you candy."

"*Mom* always brought me candy."

"I made the bank lady give us extra," Jacob said, shoving his hands into his pockets. "She'd only give it to Mom in case I was pulling her leg."

"That was you?"

"That was me."

A claw of fear tore through him, the way it always did when he realized Jacob was going to die. Someday he would let that fear take hold of him and do its worst, but not today. He had a job to do, and that required killing the fear. But how? Maybe fear was like fire. Maybe it died without oxygen. He held his breath until black dots began to dance in front of his eyes.

"Ezra," Jacob said. "We don't have to do this."

He let out his breath in a rush.

It didn't work.

Nothing did.

The fear was there and it wasn't going away.

"It's already done," he said.

§

THE RARE BOOK & Manuscript Room was at the end of a long corridor. An easel in the doorway held a blown-up version of the flyer from the mail. As he watched, a blonde woman dashed out of the room, one hand over her mouth. She hurried next door into a bathroom.

"That's her," Jacob said. "I remember her."

"Keep walking."

"She looked scared."

"I said keep walking."

"Why is she scared?"

"Global warming. How the hell should I know?"

"Promise we won't hurt her."

"I can't do that."

"You can hurt other people," Jacob said. "Just not her."

He lowered his head and glared at the open door. No one in there was his friend. No one in there deserved mercy. "I'm trying to save your life. There are no rules for that."

A black man in glasses and a pinstripe suit stepped out of the room. He picked up the easel and moved it away from the door. "You're late," he said, glaring at him and then Jacob. "Take your seats."

If this is the Death Star, Ezra thought, *that's Darth Vader.* He hurried into the room, with Jacob close on his heels. Apparently the Sinners' Bible wasn't a big draw. The room was sparsely populated, with only a dozen people scattered in four rows of folding chairs. He didn't know whether to be angry or relieved. Fewer people meant fewer witnesses, but if this book was as important as they claimed, why hadn't more people shown up? Most of the attendees looked like students, dressed in jeans and sweatshirts. He counted them off in quadrants, arranging them like an orbital diagram. The blonde woman, if she returned, would make thirteen.

An uneven number, ripe for combustion.

He shuffled toward the back row, where the slacker students always sat.

Darth Vader closed the door behind them and sat in the middle row. He crossed his left leg over his right, revealing bright blue socks with the university crest woven in white. *He runs this show,* Ezra thought. *He's the one to watch out for.*

He slipped off his backpack and edged his way through the row of chairs. A woman sat alone at the far end, one black boot propped on the seat in front of her. Long dark hair fell over her shoulders. *Princess Leia,* he thought, stepping toward her.

The woman stiffened.

He took another step, and her lips began to move as if she were arguing with someone.

One more step, and she turned to glare at him.

Not a princess, he thought, stopping dead in his tracks.

Her eyes were so pale a blue they looked white. He'd seen old folks with cataracts whose milky eyes looked like that—but she could definitely see him. Her stare froze him to the spot, as cold as Jacob's touch.

He dropped his backpack and sat where he was. Jacob eased into the chair beside him, flexing the fingers of his right hand. *Shit,* he thought. *He's lost feeling again.*

"Stay with me," he whispered. "I'm gonna need you in a few minutes."

Jacob nodded, his face tight in a grimace of pain.

Ezra gritted his teeth. This was going to be harder than he thought.

CHAPTER TWELVE

The fire sputtered. Sparks flew out like cannon balls, bursting orange and then red as they fell to the floor. He stomped one out with his boot and pulled his cloak tightly around him. Everything had gone against him.

First, they had boarded his boat.

Second, they had taken his cross. It had come from tomb of Edward the Confessor, plucked from the saint's resting place by a chorister in Westminster Abbey and presented to him in 1685, the year of his brother's death and his accession to the throne.

Third, they had hauled him off said boat to this dark and dreadful inn, where someone recognized his long nose and thin lips. A seaman, who remembered him as Lord High Admiral, the Duke of York.

James II, King of England, looked at the traitor who knelt before him. In place of a right eye, the man had a patch of reddened skin, shining like silk. Apparently, he had been spotted by the one man without the capacity to spot much of anything. There was more than chance in it—no one's luck was that terrible.

"Forgive me, Your Highness," the man said.

But there was no time for that. "Bring me paper and ink," he said. "Now." The man scuttled away and he flung himself into a chair beside the fire.

How many times would he be forced to flee his own subjects? As a boy, when his father was still alive, he had escaped Oliver Cromwell's guards by disguising himself as a little girl while playing hide-and-seek with his siblings. Now he would be forced to try again, for the rabid heretics in London were calling for him to stand trial, as his father had. His father would have said it was God's will. But why would God will a king to die, when that king had been anointed in His holy sacrament? Did God change His mind about them, the way some of them changed their minds about Him?

No. There was one true God and one true Faith.

If the people of England could not accept it, they would burn in hell. It was that simple.

But oh, how they hated him for being a Catholic.

Oh, how they hated him for marrying a Catholic.

And oh, how they hated him for baptizing his son, the Prince of Wales, as a Catholic. They hated it so much that they believed the lies his daughters spread about him—that his darling boy was a changeling, a substitute for a stillborn. They would believe anything to justify the crimes they wished to commit. They had taken his capital and given it to his daughter Mary and her husband, that Dutch Abortion, William of Orange. As if the people could choose their monarch. As if God did not decide who was born to be a king.

But Mary had let them do it.

His Mary, the gentle girl named for her great-great-grandmother, Mary Stuart. She had betrayed him, all so that her heartless husband would smile upon her. She craved his affection more than was healthy.

The army had gone over to the Dutch Abortion without hesitation. So had Anne, the daughter he sheltered and cherished after her sister went to Holland. She had fled under cover of night without so much as a farewell. His treasonous daughters, heretics though they were, were still bound by the commandment to honor thy father and mother, were they not?

"Revile and betray, more like," he muttered.

There was no one left he could trust.

God had rescinded His favor.

It was the only explanation.

But what had he done to deserve it?

He had violated the sacrament of marriage, but so had his brother and grandfather and the people loved them for it. He had violated his conscience in allowing both of his girls, Mary and Anne, to be raised in the Anglican faith. Was that his greatest sin? But he had done it to please the people, at his brother's request—at his *king's* request. Ought he to have refused?

"Paper and ink, Your Majesty," the traitorous seaman said, holding out the proffered items.

He snatched them from the man's grip. He would write a letter to each of them, those cursed daughters who would burn in hell for their disloyalty. He balanced the inkwell on his leg and scrawled out two missives. *My son, your brother, lives...and you cast us both aside because we adhere to the one True Faith. You are harlots, sinners, and you shall be cast aside on the Day of Judgment. If only my enemies had cursed me, I could have borne it.*

A shout went up outside.

He paused, his quill dripping ink like blood.

Was that William of Orange, come to bring him to London in chains, to try him and execute him as his father had been tried and executed by Cromwell? "By God, you will not," he hissed. " 'For I repent that I gave my daughter unto him, for he sought to slay me.'"

He looked over his shoulder.

They hadn't found the coronation ring and handful of diamonds in his breeches. Perhaps he could bribe that one-eyed trull to close his functioning orb for just a moment. Neither had they found the small brown Bible tucked in the pocket of his cloak. He'd kept it near him ever since he found it on his brother's bedside table, the night of Charles's death. He had recognized his mother's handwriting inside it, and added his brother's name to the cursed list of Stuart dead.

Who, he wondered, would add his name? His faithless daughters?

He pulled the Bible from his cloak and left it on the table. "Give this to my bitch of a daughter," he said. "Mary will know what to do with it."

CHAPTER THIRTEEN

Natalie knew the man five seats down from her wasn't a student. He was trying hard to look like one, but his backpack didn't have any books in it and his sweatshirt was too small. Why would someone dress up like a student to attend a lecture on the Sinners' Bible? *Who is this guy?* she asked, waiting for Belial to chime in. But the angel had pulled his wings over his head and sank into the recesses of her occipital lobe, still angry at her for refusing to talk about the Stuart curse.

Fine, she thought. *I'll figure it out myself.*

She slouched in her seat and held up a hank of hair, as if she were looking for split ends. Through the shafts of hair, she stared at him. He had a deep tan and shaggy blond hair, uncut for years, just like hers. It flattened in a circle just above his ears.

The tense planes of his face reminded her of some of the kids she'd seen in shrinks' offices as a child. They never held their mothers' hands because they knew it wouldn't help. Not with what was waiting for them on the other side of the door—the needle pricks, the strobe lights, the ice baths, the interrogations. Some things made you grow up fast.

She shifted her gaze to the big man beside him. He looked a few years older, in his late twenties. Square-jawed with a shaved head and broad shoulders, he looked like a linebacker for one of the teams that played bowl games on New Year's Day. He flexed his fingers periodically and seemed uncomfortable, shifting in his seat. He had on a thick winter coat, unbuttoned to reveal a shirt and sweater beneath it.

Neither looked like the type to be interested in religious conflict in 17th century England. Unlike the other students, they didn't have notebooks and pens ready.

Belial, she thought. *Why are they here?*

But the angel still didn't answer her.

Finally, Crawford strode to the front of the room. He looked at the clock with a dramatic sigh and drummed his fingers on the lectern. "Ten seconds," he said, looking straight at her.

She stared back at him, determined to give him nothing. In her lap, where he couldn't see it, she dug her fingernails into her palm. *Son of a bitch,* she thought. *Beth, stop throwing up and get in here.*

But her sister didn't appear, and Crawford cleared his throat. "Good evening," he said. "We're here tonight for the first public viewing of our latest acquisition. The Sinners' Bible is an extremely rare book, and we're privileged to have a copy in our collection. To kick things off, our Acting Associate

Librarian, Avi Druckman, will explain how this Bible's famous typographical errors came to be. Avi, will you stand up for a moment?"

Avi stood and waved, a sheepish grin on his face. "Hi, I'm Avi. Follow us on Facebook."

Crawford glowered at him. "You may be seated."

Avi sat.

"You'll also hear about the turbulent history of Stuart England. Professor Elizabeth Brandon will explain why the battle between Catholics and Protestants was still a problem long after the deaths of the decidedly Catholic Mary Tudor and the decidedly Protestant Elizabeth I." Crawford glanced from side to side. "Professor Brandon, will you stand up for a moment?"

Beth, she pleaded. *Get your ass in here.*

In the silence, a toilet flushed nearby. The pipes rattled in the wall, and a pair of heels clacked into the hallway outside. Beth flung open the door, her red lipstick feathered around the edges.

"Professor Brandon, so good of you to join us." Crawford pulled off his glasses. "Let's hope our audience doesn't take your tardiness as an indication of your disdain, either for them or our subject matter."

She watched Beth gulp and pull the door shut behind her. Her sister had faced Russian *spetsnaz* fighters with less internal pyrotechnics, but Crawford's disapproval reduced her to a blushing, stammering undergrad. He knew it, and he used it against her.

She fixed him in her sights. "If she's nervous, it's because she wants to do a good job, which is an indication of vulnerability and humanity. If you don't know what that means, I'm sure Avi has a really old dictionary in here somewhere."

An Asian girl in front of her gasped.

Crawford tilted his head to glare at her over the rim of his glasses. *Only assholes and supervillains glare at people over the rims of their glasses*, she thought.

Suddenly, the right side of her head began to tingle.

She turned her head slowly.

The blond man in the blue sweatshirt was smiling at her.

"What are you looking at?" she snapped, crossing her arms over her chest and turning her attention to the presentation.

§

"As a result," Avi said, "there are rumors that the typographical errors in the Sinners' Bible were the product of sabotage. If the type had been laid out and left unguarded, anyone could have broken into the shop and altered the verse in question. It was unlikely the type would have been checked again before printing."

The Asian girl raised her hand. "Wouldn't it have been easier to burn down their shop?"

"It would have," he said, "if the saboteur wanted to put Barker and Lucas out of business."

"That isn't what they wanted," she said, as she glared at the back of Crawford's skull. "Why put them out of business when public humiliation is so much more effective?"

Two rows ahead of her, Beth's head sank to her chest.

Avi glanced at the clock and breathed a sigh of relief. "It looks like my time's up. Who's ready to see one of the rarest Bibles in the world?"

No one moved or spoke.

"I'm gonna need you to contain that enthusiasm for one more minute." He pulled a set of keys from his pocket and unlocked a door behind the lectern. A moment later, he wheeled out a metal cart with a clear plastic lid. Beneath the lid lay the open copy of the Sinners' Bible. Judging by the number of unturned pages, she guessed it was open to the typo in Exodus.

Belial shuddered and raised his head.

Don't you start, she thought. *Not until Beth's talk is over. That was the deal.*

You need me, the angel said.

No one needs you, she thought, sliding her fingers under her sleeve and digging her nails into her scar.

Your sister needs me.

I said—

That boy needs me, too.

She stopped.

In her peripheral vision, she saw the blond man stand up and pull a gun from his waistband. It had a silencer attached to the muzzle. "Everyone stay where you are," he said. "If you move, you die."

CHAPTER FOURTEEN

"*Send her away*," Mary Stuart groaned. "She's eavesdropping on me."

Beside her sickbed, Thomas Tenison, the Archbishop of Canterbury, leaned closer. "Ma'am, whom do you wish to be sent away?"

"That Popish nurse. Behind the screen, at the head of the bed. Don't you see her?"

Tenison shook his head. "There is no one there, Your Majesty."

"She is," Mary whispered. "Why can't you see her?"

The nurse was listening, as she had been seventeen years earlier, while her sister Anne was abed with smallpox. Their father, James, had paid the woman to spy on them. He wanted a sign that one or both of his daughters might show favor to the Popish religion.

"Never," she whispered.

She glanced at the foot of her bed. All around her stood men and women of the court—ministers, servants, doctors, clergymen, and ladies-in-waiting. The ones who had never had smallpox had been given leave to go. She did not want their deaths on her conscience. That was burdened enough already.

"I did not want it," she said, turning her head away. "That was never what I wanted. Do you hear me?"

"Your Majesty, I beg of you, save your strength."

For what? she wondered. *Confession is all that is left to me.*

It had been almost six years since Parliament read out the people's grievances with her father, James II, and asked her and her husband, William, to redress them. "It hath been found by experience," they said, "to be inconsistent with the safety and welfare of this Protestant kingdom to be governed by a popish prince." So she had accepted the crown while standing in the pouring rain outside the Banqueting House at Whitehall—the same place they had raised a scaffold to cut off her grandfather's head.

Her father had written to her afterward. *If you are crowned while I and the Prince of Wales are living, the curses of an angry father will fall on you, as well as those of a God who commands obedience to parents.*

"But the people offered us the crown," she whispered. "Beneath the great canopy of state."

"Your Majesty?" Tenison glanced at the canopy above her bed.

"I never wanted it!"

"You must stay calm, Your Majesty." The Archbishop took her hand and she had not the strength to remove it from his grasp. "The people pray for your recovery."

Her people…so barbarous in manner and so good in heart. She felt ashamed that they were not the reason she had betrayed her father. No, she had broken a Biblical commandment and betrayed her own blood for quite a different reason.

"His eyes," she breathed. "Never have they shone as they did in that moment."

"Your Majesty, shall I call the doctor?"

"He needed me, Tenison. In that moment, he needed me."

She was a Stuart, the daughter of the king and the rightful heir to the throne. If she had not accepted Parliament's offer, William could have taken the throne—but he would have had to fight for it. In that moment, she was the only person in the world who could give William what he wanted. And she'd done it, damning her father and half-brother in the process. "It was supposed to make us happy," she said. "Why didn't it make us happy?"

Before the days of fighting and revolution, she and William had lived in peace at Honselaersdijck, riding and gardening and drinking tea in her yellow and violet study. She wished it had been her destiny to live quietly there for all her days, but God saw fit to deny her that dream. Then He had taken the only other consolation she might have had—a child, dead within her womb. There had never been another.

"I am adrift," she whispered. "God wills me to be detached from this life."

He had cursed her as surely as He had cursed her father and grandfather. Or had she cursed herself when she disobeyed His commandment to honor her father? Perhaps it had been destined from the moment her father named her after that other Mary Stuart, her great-great-grandmother, who had gone to her death a foolish, lustful Popish queen.

"But a queen with a son," she said, fingers grasping the bedsheets tightly. The lack hurt deep in her chest, pulsing with life like a living thing. It was all she had given birth to, in the end. Without a child, her sister Anne would reign upon William's death.

Her sister, who hated her. Her sister, who could not even be roused to speak to her on her deathbed.

She remembered the days of their youth, when they had played with dolls at Richmond together. What had happened to turn Anne's devoted heart black with envy? "We are a cursed family," she moaned. "In all this, I see the hand of God."

"Please, Your Majesty," Tenison said. He waved to a serving woman, who mopped her forehead with a wet rag.

"Write my name," she said, grabbing the Archbishop's hand. "In the book that catalogues my family's misery."

Tenison narrowed his eyes. "What book, Your Majesty?"

"My family's Bible." She closed her eyes. "Write my name beneath the others. See that my sister receives it after I am gone. Her name will end there, too."

A wave of heat crested over her. This disease made it hard to think, hard to see.

Very well, she thought. *I will close my eyes and dream of Holland.*

CHAPTER FIFTEEN

Natalie looked at the man with the gun and a jolt of fear shot through her veins. The door was closed, and he had a silencer. He could shoot them all, if he wanted. *Belial,* she mouthed. *Wake up.*

The gunman aimed the pistol at Avi. "What else is behind that door?"

Avi held up his hands. "It's a s—storage room. Shelves and manuscripts."

"Get in."

Avi nodded and stepped backward.

"Wait," the gunman said. "Your phone. Put it on the lectern."

She tilted her head. Whoever this guy was, he wasn't someone she'd have pegged to use the word *lectern.* Her eyes flickered toward Beth, but her sister was facing forward, stock-still.

The gunman moved to the front of the room. "You," he said, aiming at an Asian girl who was holding up her hands and hyperventilating with fear. "Into the storage room." He proceeded through the first two rows of folding chairs, directing everyone to drop their phones on the lectern and proceed into the storage room.

Belial, she thought. *He's coming to Beth. What do I do?*

I thought you wanted me to go away, the angel said.

The gunman held the pistol with an easy grip, his index finger laced over the trigger. "You," he said, stopping in front of Beth's chair. He held the muzzle inches from her forehead, then flashed a gap-toothed smile. "Stay awhile."

She let out a shaky breath.

What did it mean that he'd singled Beth out? They all knew she was supposed to present next. Maybe he wanted to ask her something about the Sinners' Bible before he stole it? But Avi had already presented on the Bible itself, and the gunman had ordered him into the closet. So what did he want with Beth?

Think.

She gulped and looked at the floor. The legs of the gunman's jeans puddled above the tongues of his canvas skate shoes, as if he normally wore boots. But the jeans were the wrong cut and color for a skater—too dark an indigo, stonewashed, too close-fitting. If he wasn't a student and he wasn't a skater, who was he?

The gunman proceeded through the last two rows, sending everyone into the storage room except for herself,

Crawford, and the big man he'd come in with. When the last student, a skinny kid in a Bill Murray T-shirt, had shuffled into the storage room, he leaned against the door and let his gun arm fall to his side. "Guy with glasses," he said. "Give me the keys."

They jangled as Avi tossed them into the air.

The gunman caught them neatly in his left hand. "You make any noise, and someone out here dies. Nod if you understand."

"You're locking us in?" a scared voice asked. "What about oxygen?"

"Hold your breath." He kicked the door shut and locked it, tossing the keys onto the lectern. Then he stepped toward the first row of folding chairs, propping one leg on a chair seat. "This won't take long if you cooperate. There's no reason we can't all get what we want." He used the gun as a pointer, aiming the muzzle at her. "You, with the weird eyes. Come here."

Memories of Russia cascaded over her, a nightmare fabric woven with guns and blood. There, she'd had Constantine to protect her. Now, there was no one. *I can't do this,* she thought.

You are strong, Belial said. *And I am strong, too.*

She forced herself not to look at Beth as she stood up. She didn't want to do anything that would give him something to use against them. "All right, I'm coming. Don't hurt anyone."

He watched with a bemused expression as she moved toward him. Strands of shaggy blond hair fell over his eyes and he made no move to sweep them away. "Your eyes always looked like that?"

"Every damn day of my life."

"Were you scared the first time you saw yourself in a mirror?"

"I'm still scared today. What do you want me to do?"

"Open the lid on that cart and bring me the book."

"Why can't you do it?"

"I asked you first, and I'm the one holding the gun."

"Scared you'll leave fingerprints?"

"Just bring me the goddamn book."

She frowned. What was the point of worrying about fingerprints when they'd all seen his face? Did that mean he planned to kill them, leaving no witnesses? But how was she supposed to stop him? The pair of scissors was in her bag on the floor and in the back row. She had no weapon and no way of fighting back.

You have a weapon, Belial said. *The same one you've always had.*

She gulped. That was exactly what she was afraid of. She couldn't forget what Belial had done last year, in the motel room in South San Francisco. He'd begged her to give him control, and she'd done it to save her own life...at a tremendous cost. What if something like that happened again? Even if the Stuart curse wasn't real, Belial was, and she was far more scared of him.

I want that book, the angel said. *The curse is alive inside it.*

She focused on the gunman. "You don't want this book."

A ghost of a smile flickered on his lips. "A Jedi mind trick? Really?"

"It's not a—" She stopped and took a deep breath. "Trust me. You don't want this book."

"It's the only reason I'm here. Bring it to me."

I want it, Belial said, extending the arch of his wings. *I need to touch it.*

You don't even have fingers, she thought.

I have you, the angel replied.

"Open it," the gunman said. "Now."

Open it, Belial said. *Now.*

"Natalie, what the hell are you doing?" Beth said. "Give him the book."

She bit her lip until tears stung her eyes and she tasted blood. "I can't…something bad will happen."

"Damn right it will." The gunman slid his finger through the trigger guard. "Jacob, lock the door."

The big man in the back row stood up and moved to the door.

"Wait!" Crawford raised his hand, as if he were a student in class. A sheen of sweat glistened on his forehead. "Young man, that lock triggers a silent alarm."

"You're lying."

"This is my university. I wrote the protocol and procedures myself."

"Did you?" The gunman kicked aside folding chairs as he strode toward Crawford. He grabbed Crawford's throat with his left hand and pointed at the door with the gun in his right. "That bolt doesn't even touch the frame. There's no contact to break, and no silent alarm. The next time you use a Parthian shot, you better be damn sure there's an arrow in that bow of yours." He dragged the gun across Crawford's lips, as if painting on a smile. "Jacob, please lock the door."

The man named Jacob slid the bolt home and blocked the door with his body.

Bring me the book now, Belial said. *Let me touch the pages cursed with their blood.*

"It's not real," she whispered.

I am an angel of the Lord, and your constant companion for twenty-two years. Do you still believe that only the things you can see are real?

"Don't hurt them," she said. "Not through me."

The gunman released Crawford and whipped his head toward her. "What did you say?"

She held up both hands in surrender. "Don't take that book. I can't explain why, I just know something terrible will happen if you do."

"Ezra," Jacob called. "Come on, man. Just get the book and let's go."

"Don't!" She blinked back the hot tears building behind her lashes. "I think someone will die if that happens. I think I might hurt them."

Ezra narrowed his gray eyes at her. "What in holy hell are you talking about?"

"I don't want to hurt anyone. I don't want anyone to die." She grabbed his arm. "What if it's you?"

He pointed the gun at Beth. "What if it's her?"

The book, Belial said. *Get it now.* He dragged a wing down the side of her skull. Every tiny feather point felt like a solar flare, burning her skull from the inside out. She shrieked and dropped to her knees, holding her head in her hands.

"Shut up!" Ezra flung himself down beside her and clamped his left hand over her mouth. "What the hell's wrong with you?" His right hand, still holding the gun, snaked around her waist and pulled her against him.

"Let her go!" Beth cried. "She's sick. She has epilepsy."

Crawford gasped. "Is this true, Ms. Brandon?"

That old lie again, Belial said.

Tears streamed from her eyes as the flares of pain ebbed and flowed. It would hurt to speak. It would hurt to shake her head. But she had to stop them both—Belial and Ezra.

"Epilepsy," Ezra said, his wide gray eyes searching hers.

"Let me help her," Beth said. "I know what to do."

Ezra ignored Beth, speaking only to her. "Why is she lying? It's something in your head, all right, but it's not epilepsy. You didn't lose consciousness. You didn't bite your tongue. You didn't arch your back." He pulled his hand from her mouth. "What do you really have?"

"P—peanut butter," she said. "Your hands smell like peanut butter."

"Listen, both of you." Crawford stood up slowly. "She clearly needs a doctor. Just go, right now, and we'll get her to a hospital. Don't make this any worse."

"Worse?" Ezra said. "How could things get worse? Do you think I'm here because I give a shit about some old book?"

From the corner of her eye, she saw Crawford move one hand toward his jacket pocket. "Don't," she moaned.

But it was too late.

Ezra raised his right hand and fired.

The bullet struck Crawford in the chest. The cell phone fell out of his hand as he collapsed onto the next row of folding chairs. The crash echoed like a firecracker in a tin can.

"No!" Beth screamed, scrambling toward him.

Jacob leapt for her, catching her around the waist and clamping a hand over her mouth.

He is gentle, Belial said. *But it is too late.*

Panic dimmed the pain as she scrambled in Ezra's arms. "Tell him to let her go!"

Ezra wrenched her shoulders to the ground, leaning on them to keep her pressed to the floor. The gun in his right hand dug into the hollow above her collarbone. "What do you really have?"

"I d—don't know."

"You had a headache. I saw it. I saw *you.*"

Beth let out a strangled sob and Jacob tightened his grip on her.

Cold, the angel said. *His hands are so cold.*

"Cold," she moaned. "His hands are so cold."

A shock went through Ezra's body. She felt it move through him, originating in his gut.

I am the weapon, she thought. *I've always been the weapon.*

Very good, little one. Now tell him that your sister can feel the cold, spreading through her veins like ice.

"But it's more than his hands, isn't it?" she said. "Maybe his whole body is cold where it touches you."

She looked up into Ezra's eyes. The soul inside them was old, like hers, calcified into hardness from break after break after break. She remembered the way he'd said the other man's name—it was the same way she said Beth's name. Suddenly, she understood why Jacob wore so many layers of clothing, why he was cold, why Ezra was so interested in her head…

"You love him," she said, "but you can't save him."

He pushed down on her shoulders. "You don't know what you're talking about!"

"Love is strong, but other things are strong, too." She slid her fingers down her right arm and then her left, reaching for the sleeves of her shirt. She pulled them up to reveal her scars, two opaque trails that looked like curdled milk.

I told you I was sorry, Belial said.

Ezra gasped. "What the fuck is wrong with you?" His eyes traced each scar, lingering on the puckered ends, tiny starburst nubs of pinched flesh. "Some people fight so hard for what you tried to throw away."

"It wasn't just me this thing was killing."

He held one finger over her wrist, stopping just short of touching her. "Did it hurt?"

She bit her lip, remembering the night she'd opened her veins. Dante had asked her to do it, but that wasn't why she'd obeyed. "No," she lied.

"Goddamn, woman. Are you brave or crazy?"

"I know how it feels to watch someone you love suffer because of something you can't control. You can't fight it, and suddenly there are two things killing you." She blinked, remembering the cold sting of the night air as it whispered to her open veins. "I just wanted to help one of them win."

Ezra blinked. "I want Jacob to win."

"He doesn't want this for you."

"I want him to live!"

"Maybe that's not your decision to make."

"You don't understand." Ezra shook his head. "You can't. I've been doing this all wrong."

She nodded, scraping her head against the floor.

He swung his right hand and pointed the gun at Beth. "You can't understand because you don't give a shit what happens to you. But what about her? Do you give a shit about her? Bring me that book or she gets a bullet in the brain."

You cannot let them have it, Belial said. *It does not belong to them.*

She gritted her teeth. Every muscle in her body wanted to contract, to curl up in a ball to protect herself. But a ball wouldn't save her from a bullet, and it wouldn't help Beth.

Seth had a math test next week, full of polynomials.

He needed her. Beth needed her. And she needed them.

I am the weapon, she thought.

She forced a nervous smile to her lips, feeling the dry skin split as it stretched. "You asked if I was brave or crazy, but it's neither of those things."

"What the hell else is there?"

"There's an angel inside my head." She reached for his right hand and guided it to her temple, placing the muzzle of the gun against her hairline. "He's already pissed at me. But let's see what happens if we make him really mad."

"Natalie, no!" Beth cried. She stomped on Jacob's insole and elbowed him in the gut.

Jacob wheezed and let go, clutching his midsection.

Ezra swore and wrenched the gun from her grasp.

That second was all her sister needed.

Beth dove, landing hard on Ezra's right arm.

He roared in pain as she crushed his wrist against the floor. He tried to pull his hand out from under her, but it didn't work. So he rolled toward Beth and launched his left fist into the side of her head. Her sister's limp form slumped over his elbow.

Ezra jerked his arm out from under Beth's body and scuttled backward, aiming the gun at her sister's head.

"No!" Natalie screamed. "Not her!"

Suddenly, a blue-shirted blur flew past her. Jacob's breaths were short and shallow. His ruddy face had gone pale. He fell to one knee in front of Beth. "I asked you not to hurt her."

"And I told you I'd do this my way!" Ezra said.

It is too late, little one, Belial said. *His brother cannot be saved.*

"Ezra," she said, crawling toward him and holding out her hand. "Look at me, please."

Ezra turned his back on her.

"You love your brother. I understand that better than anyone. But Belial says it's too late." Her gaze flickered up to Jacob. "I'm sorry."

"I know," he said.

A siren rang out across the quad.

Beth moaned and struggled to sit up. Jacob touched her arm gently. She looked up at him and his face softened as he watched her hair fall across her cheek. "I never meant for this to happen," he said.

Then he walked to the metal rolling cart, unlatched the plastic lid, and pulled out the book. A red ribbon lay across the open page. He looked at it for a moment, then slammed it closed. "All this trouble over a damn book," he said.

CHAPTER SIXTEEN

OCTOBER 28, 1708
KENSINGTON PALACE, LONDON

"*Please, Your Majesty,*" the serving girl said. "You must leave this room. He cannot be seen to properly with you here."

Anne Stuart, Queen of England, leaned across the bed and kissed her dead husband's lips.

"Your Majesty, the Duchess of Marlborough awaits you in your bedchamber. Don't you wish to greet her?"

"I am where I belong!" she cried, rounding on the girl. "Get out, and leave me be."

The girl's cheeks reddened, but she curtsied and did as she was told.

Anne turned back to George. "What will I do without you?" she said, sniffling as the tears streamed down her face. She stroked his cheek, resting her fingertips at the corner of his mouth.

Seventeen times her cursed womb had grown quick with his child, and seventeen times it had ended in blood and pain and the closing of tiny eyes. If God did not wish her to have children, why had He allowed their hopes to rise so many times? Even the old drunks in the taverns grew tired of kicking the dogs at their feet.

But God did not tire of tormenting the Stuart family.

Perhaps He wanted to be sure there were no more of them.

He had achieved that with certainty now.

James, the first Stuart king of England, had married Anne of Denmark. Now there was only she, surely the last of them, weeping over the body of her husband, Anne's great-nephew. The symmetry was as beautiful as the Great Court at Blenheim. When she was dead, they would say about her what they had said about her sister, Mary: "Go, see now this cursed woman, and bury her, for she is a king's daughter."

Even the common priests in the pulpit knew her family was cursed.

What they did not know was that while Mary may have disobeyed the Fifth Commandment and taken the crown from their father, it was she who had hardened Mary's heart against him. Upon her sister's death, the former Archbishop of Bath and Wells had said, "I hope the surviving Princess will consider, and take warning, and repent, lest God be provided to cut her life as short as her sister's."

But she had not.

She was glad that her father's son, her stepbrother, was excluded from the line of succession. The English people did not want a Catholic monarch, and in any case, if the throne had gone back to her father and his Catholic children, it would have made her sin and Mary's sin all for naught.

It had to be worth something to be borne.

She looked at the small, brown Bible resting at the foot of the bed. She had clutched it in terror as George struggled to fill his lungs with air. *Please*, she had prayed. *Please don't take him from me. Of all the names written here, he played no part in their affairs. He is nothing to You. Leave him be, I beg of You.*

Five minutes later, he was dead.

So there was her answer, a private communication from the Divine.

"George," she sobbed, laying her cheek against his breast.

The bedchamber door creaked open behind her.

"I told you to leave," she snapped at the serving girl.

"Mrs. Morley," said a familiar voice. It was the nickname by which she was known only to Sarah Churchill.

"Go away," she said. "You are not wanted here."

"Mrs. Morley, you must come away now. It is time." Sarah strode up to her and placed her arms around her. But she did not wrap her arms around her for the sake of comfort. Sarah pulled, attempting to dislodge her from George's side.

Anne struck out at her, beating Sarah's soft arms with her fists. "No! I cannot leave him!"

"We are going to St. James's," Sarah said, ducking the blows with ease. "It is for the best."

"You cannot make me!"

"Then why do you plead like a child?" Sarah pulled at her shoulders one more time. "Oh, have it your way," she said, letting go with a huff. "Two more minutes, then?"

"No," Anne gasped, clutching the bedclothes. "It is too soon."

"You are a queen, my dear. Your sorrow is secondary to your duty. And your duty awaits at St. James's."

"I want to be with him."

"You have been with him for twenty-five years."

"Then I would be with him for twenty-six!"

As soon as she left the room, they would take George away. They would shut him up in a tomb and she would never see his face again. This was the last moment she would have with him, to stroke his dear face and kiss his dear lips. Why could they not grant it to her in peace? Did they not understand that part of her would die here, too?

She raised her head from his breast and reached for the Bible resting at the foot of the bed. "Bring me ink and quill," she murmured. "I must write my name now."

Sarah raised one delicate eyebrow, but moved to the bureau and brought her the items she wanted. "And after this, shall I call the carriage?"

"After this," she said, opening the back cover. "You will leave me."

She ran her fingers over the names of the Stuarts who had preceded her in death. Some meant little to her, like the name of her French great-grandfather, Henri. Others...

Fresh tears spilled from her eyes as her fingers pressed against the name at the bottom of the list: William, dead before his twelfth birthday, the only one of her children to live that long. She had written his name with such great anguish that her quill dug into the paper, etching it rather than writing it. "Mama is with you still," she said, dipping the quill and writing her own name beneath his.

"Whatever are you doing?" Sarah asked, looking over her shoulder.

"Writing in the book of the dead." She blew on the ink to help it dry.

"A bit premature, don't you think?"

She looked up at Sarah, once the greatest love in her life—a friend where she had had none, a heart open to her when all others had been closed. But too much had passed between them for their relationship to be a source of comfort. Tears and jealousy had bound and broken a love that used to roam unfettered. "When I breathe my last, none will be there to write my name in this book." She slammed the book shut. "So I have done it myself."

"Now may we depart for St. James's?"

"Call the chambermaid, please, Mrs. Freeman."

Sarah's face softened for a moment when she heard her own private nickname, and she did as she was asked. In a moment, the same white-faced girl stood in front of her who had urged her to leave poor George's side a few moments ago.

"Y—your Majesty," the girl said, dropping into a stiff curtsy.

"Take this," she said, holding out the Bible. "You will burn it on the day I die."

The girl blinked. "But it is a Bible, Your Majesty."

"Yes, it is."

"I cannot burn the word of God!"

"You can if your sovereign orders you to do it."

"But surely you will not die for many years, Your Majesty."

She met the girl's frightened brown eyes. "Then you had better live at least five minutes longer than I. That is an order. Do you understand?"

"Y—yes, Your Majesty."

She dismissed the girl, and watched her hurry away with the book clutched to her chest.

"Do you suppose she'll actually burn it?" Sarah asked, carrying the ink and quill back to the bureau.

"I pity her if she does not." She turned her back on Sarah and reached for George's hand. She placed a kiss on his palm and laced her fingers through his, holding their joined fingers to her cheek. "But I will be dead and beyond its reach. George will be there to greet me, and I will not spoil our reunion with talk of unhappy things."

CHAPTER SEVENTEEN

MARCH 2014
SAN FRANCISCO, CALIFORNIA

Jacob held the book out to Beth. "Take this," he said softly. "I never wanted it."

"Jacob, stop," Ezra said. "We have to go now."

Natalie kept her eyes on Jacob's face. He didn't look at his brother. He kept his clear blue eyes on Beth's face. "I only came because I saw your picture on the flyer. I asked him not to hurt you."

Beth sat up slowly. A bright red patch of skin glowed on the side of her face. "I don't even know you," she said, blinking tear-filled eyes. "But thank you."

"Don't blame him for this. It's my fault."

Take the book, Belial said. *Keep it safe. Do it now.*

She crawled toward Jacob on her hands and knees. Tiny particles of dirt and sand ground against her palms and she grimaced. "Beth, let me take it," she said.

When her sister nodded, she slid the Bible from Jacob's outstretched hand.

As soon as she touched it, a stream of images flooded her brain. A head falling onto bloodstained straw. A woman's chin coated with blood and black mucus. Two women in silk and lace, holding each other and crying. A little boy's purple lips, drawing his last breath. The book was a part of them. They were a part of the book. They were bound up in each other, forever, and their souls were crushing her.

"Belial, make it stop," she whispered.

They had such promise, Belial said. *If only they could have been stronger.*

She clutched the book to her chest and curled her feet to avoid the red puddle spreading from beneath Crawford's body. "No blood," she whispered. "No more blood."

In the single moment she was off-balance, Ezra lunged for her. He grabbed one arm and jerked her toward him, pressing the muzzle of the gun to her wrist.

"Nat!" Beth cried.

"Don't you look at her," Ezra said. "Just look at me."

She gulped, keeping her eyes focused on his. *I am the weapon*, she thought. *I am fire and gunpowder encased in flesh.*

"Do you know what this is?" Ezra dragged the muzzle of the gun along the length of her scar. "This is proof that someone fought for you. My brother deserves that, too."

White half-moons hooded his fingers where they dug into her. She tried to jerk her arm back, but he held on tight. "Of course he does. But sometimes we can't…" She shook her head. "Belial said it's too late."

"It's not!" Ezra cried. "Not as long as he's breathing, and that means I can't stop trying!"

"Ezra." Jacob gripped his brother's shoulder. "Come on. Put the gun down."

"Not until she gives me that book."

"I'll give you the money," she said. "As much as you need."

Ezra laughed, a strained high-pitched cackle. "You got a hundred thousand dollars on you, right here, right now? 'Cause we're leaving tonight, and I need that book to fix things. I promised him I would." He sniffed and raised the gun to her forehead with a shaking hand. "I don't have a choice because he doesn't have a choice. The good, the bad, everything, we share it."

"A covalent bond," she whispered.

"Yeah." He nodded and wiped his nose with his sleeve. "It's like that."

"Don't do this," Beth sobbed. "Nat, just give them the book."

I won't let you do that, Belial said. *It isn't yours to give.*

Ezra's finger twitched on the trigger. The barrel was cold on her forehead. Her sister's arms were warm. "I love you, Beth," she said.

Ezra's finger began to move.

She closed her eyes.

A breath of air rushed alongside her ear.

The shot flew wide, pinging into the wall.

She opened her eyes and saw Jacob snap his brother's wrist. Ezra screamed and Jacob slid the gun from his grip. It lay in his palm and he studied it.

"No!" Ezra bellowed, cradling his wrist.

His brother hefted the pistol and slipped his finger through the trigger guard.

"Jacob, no." Beth sobbed and held out her hand. "Please don't do this. Talk to me."

"Tell them that was me," he said, pointing at Crawford's body. "And tell them my brother belongs in a place like this."

Then he closed his eyes, put the gun in his mouth, and pulled the trigger.

CHAPTER EIGHTEEN

zra dove. He stretched out his hands to keep Jacob's head from hitting the floor. He ignored the pain from his broken wrist and hefted his brother's bulk into his arms, fingers roving over his chest and throat as if there were something he could do.

A vicious splatter of red painted the walls, the floor, the lectern, everything.

"I was going to fix it," he said, rocking his brother's torso. "Why didn't you trust me?"

The wail of the sirens was getting louder.

The gun lay on the floor, on the other side of Jacob's body.

The woman named Natalie clasped the Bible to her chest. Her face and arms were splattered with Jacob's blood. "You made this happen, Belial," she whispered, her blue-white eyes wide and full of water.

The woman named Beth pressed herself to her feet and stumbled toward the lectern. She picked up the key ring. She was going to let out all his hostages.

None of that mattered anymore.

He turned his head so he wouldn't have to see the blood pouring from the back of Jacob's head. Something smelled like meat and metal and pepper and sweat. At home, it smelled like bananas. They ripened on the counter and made the whole goddamn trailer stink. He hated bananas. He only bought them for the potassium, for Jacob. What the hell would he do with the bunch that wasn't ripe yet? Why the hell was he thinking about bananas? Why wasn't he moving, running, finding a way to fix things, like he'd promised? Every second of his life opened up before him like a black hole, an impossible distance he had no ability or wish to cover because there was nothing on the other side.

The blonde woman grabbed one of the cell phones on the lectern. She balanced it between her ear and her shoulder as she staggered toward the storage room door. "I need an ambulance!" she cried. "The Rare Book and Manuscript Room. Two men have been shot, one might still be alive."

Her hand turned a key in the lock.

The people inside flooded out.

One girl looked at Jacob's body and screamed.

He bent his head over his brother's chest. The shirt still smelled like Jacob, like wheat and soap. "I don't know what to do," he said, rocking Jacob's body. "Tell me what to do."

The farm was as good as gone. Without his brother, so was he. Assault, attempted murder, attempted robbery, carrying a concealed weapon…they'd ship him off to Lompoc or Soledad. And for what? Because a stupid girl wouldn't give up a stupid goddamn book.

"You," he snarled, raising his head and glaring at Natalie. "You did this."

Tears shone in her milk-glass eyes. "I know."

"My brother is dead because of you!"

"I know."

One of the kids from the storage room ran to the front door and pushed it, not realizing it had been locked from the inside. She screamed and pounded on the door.

"Unlock it!" the blonde woman shouted. "The latch at the top!"

A tall boy reached up and slid the manual lock. The students streamed out, some still shrieking.

The blonde woman stumbled back to them, holding her hand to her head. She stopped when she realized the gun was still on the floor.

"Take it," he said. "Shoot me if you want."

She picked it up and ejected the magazine, racking the slide with her left hand to discharge the round in the chamber. "Not high on my to-do list at the moment."

"Where'd you learn to do that?"

"I saw a bunch of Russian hit men do it."

"Who *are* you?" he asked, glancing between both women.

"No one," Natalie said.

"I don't think I believe that." He rested his hand on Jacob's chest. "You never told me what you really have. He had a stage 4 glioblastoma."

"I told you." Natalie blinked her ghostly eyes. "An angel lives inside me."

"Aren't angels supposed to save people?"

"Not this one," she said softly.

He rubbed his eyes and his nose on his sleeve. "Why couldn't you let me have the goddamn book?"

"Belial would have made me hurt someone to keep it. It's a part of the Stuart curse."

"Bullshit," he said, thinking of the doctors who'd refused to operate on Jacob. "People are the curse."

"They don't have to be." Two more tears slid down her cheeks. "The police will come."

He felt her haunted eyes on him, waiting for him to answer the unspoken question. He looked away and his gaze fell on Jacob's right hand, resting on the floor. It looked lonely, the fingers spread out over the pale tile. He picked it up and held it, like he would have if the end had come in a hospital.

"No," he finally said. "Don't you dare do that to him."

CHAPTER NINETEEN

MARCH 2014
SAN FRANCISCO, CALIFORNIA

*N*atalie *watched as* the paramedics lifted Crawford onto a backboard. One of them put on a cervical collar and hefted a bag of clear liquid. "Don't let him die," she whispered. "I'm sorry I called him an asshole and a supervillain."

He will live, Belial answered. *But he will remember.*

"I don't care." She clasped the Sinners' Bible to her chest. "Just don't let him die."

The paramedics placed the backboard on a stretcher and wheeled him out.

He thinks you have epilepsy, the angel said.

"Better than the truth."

Jacob's body lay on the floor. One of the paramedics had covered him with a white sheet after the police took Ezra. Through a window, she saw the blue strobe of a patrol car's roof lights. She turned to look at her sister, seated in a folding chair across the room, where a paramedic inspected the red patch on the side of her head. "She's okay, right?"

Yes, little one.

"He almost shot me."

The bullet would not have pierced your skull.

"Why wouldn't you just let them have the book?"

Look inside and I will show you.

She uncrossed her arms and held the book in front of her. "It looks so ordinary."

It was, until it became theirs.

She turned it over and lifted the back cover, feeling the rough grain of desiccated leather under her fingertips. There, on the left side of the page, she saw a series of names written in varying shades of black ink. The two at the top were faintest, written in a flowery hand.

Henri

Charles

Henriette

Charles

James

Mary

William

Anne

"These names…did this really belong to the Stuarts?"

I've been trying to tell you. You refused to listen.

Her fingers hovered over the first name, working backward in the genealogy. "Henrietta Maria's father. Is this her handwriting?"

You tell me, little one.

She looked at the name.

The letters were tall and thin, sharp rather than rounded, with a flourish at the top of the "h" in Henri. They bowed in the middle. "It is, isn't it? She wrote her own father's name first because she thought the curst began with him."

She bit her lip, wondering if she'd have felt the same in Henrietta Maria's shoes. Henri IV couldn't have done a better job of committing adultery if it actually *had* been one of the Ten Commandments. When Henrietta Maria saw this Bible's mistake in print, maybe it did seem like a celestial reminder of her father's sins. Maybe she even saw it as a warning. But it was a huge leap from a warning to a curse, especially when everything that happened to the Stuarts had been of their own making. Human frailty was the curse, not the sins of Henrietta Maria's father.

"There is no curse, is there, Belial?"

Look at that list and tell me something unholy does not stalk that bloodline.

"You said it yourself—if only they had been stronger. They brought it on themselves."

After all, she thought, a similar litany of terrible things had happened to Henri IV's French descendants, and no one talked about a Bourbon curse. Louis XVI was dethroned and executed, just like Charles I. Louis XV, well known for his womanizing, died of smallpox, alone and unloved. Louis XIV was almost dethroned in the Fronde, and had to watch disease stalk his bloodline, taking his children and grandchildren during his lifetime. As an old and bitter man, he left a mountain of debt and a decaying throne to his tiny great-grandson.

So was it a Stuart curse or a Bourbon curse? Who could tell, when European royal dynasties mingled so much of their blood?

Maybe, in God's eyes, they were all the same.

"Are we?" she asked. "All the same?"

The angel sighed. She felt his breath behind her eyes and a flood of goosebumps stormed down her arms. Across the room, Beth stood up and touched the side of her head gingerly. Then her sister held out her hand and offered the paramedic a bright smile and a handshake.

"No," Natalie said. "We're not all the same."

A pair of legs hurried toward her and she looked up to find Avi Druckman, his gaze locked onto the Bible in her hands. "What the hell happened out here?"

"Take it," she said, holding out the book. "There's blood on it."

He reached for the Bible and she let it slide from her grasp. "Do you believe in ghosts, Avi?"

"I believe in Maimonides." He glanced behind him, where bloodstains were seeping through the white sheet over Jacob's body. "Are you afraid this room is haunted now?"

"No. That's not what I'm afraid of." She shivered. "Where did the university get that book?"

"An auction. Someone was selling a pretty big collection."

"Who?"

Avi pushed his glasses further up the bridge of his nose. "Some guy named Sinclair. British baron, fallen on hard times or something like that. Crawford keeps an eye out for stuff like that."

It has begun, Belial said.

"What has begun?" she asked.

"Nothing," Avi said. "What are you even talking about?"

The end, the angel replied. *Next time, you will not be so lucky.*

"Lucky." Her gaze drifted back to the bloodstains on Jacob's sheet. "Is that what I am?"

Avi touched her shoulder. "Are you sure you're okay? Maybe you should talk to one of the paramedics. I'm just gonna put this in storage, where it's safe. I'll be right back."

She opened her mouth to tell him about the Stuarts, that this book was part of their story, that they'd touched it and kept it and cried with it for almost a hundred years, each believing he or she was the sinner for whom it was meant, the sinner upon whom God had focused the full power of his fury. But what did it matter when there was a dead body three feet away from her? Scholars called it the Sinners' Bible, as if it belonged to *every* sinner. But it didn't. It couldn't.

It was the Sinner's Bible.

It could only belong to one of them at a time.

Whoever possessed it was doomed to be alone in their pain. Maybe that was the real curse.

"I don't want to be alone, Avi," she whispered. "Take that thing away from me."

I am with you, little one, Belial said. *After all these years, you still don't understand that, do you?*

"I'll tell you what I understand." She looked across the room to Beth as her sister waved at the departing paramedics. "Polynomials," she said. "And covalent bonds."

The End

Author's Note

Thank you for reading! I hope you enjoyed the story.

You might be wondering how much of the historical component of this story is real. The answer is…quite a bit. There really are a few copies of the Sinner's Bible left, and they come up for auction occasionally. The typo wasn't discovered until about a year after printing, just like in Chapter One.

As for the Stuarts, I embellished several of the stories for dramatic effect. For example, although many at the time believed Henriette was poisoned, she likely died of a gastric ulcer. Similarly, the story about Charles II's deathbed conversion is a bit murky. Was he the one who requested the conversion, or was it his brother or his Catholic mistress? Was he conscious enough to know it was happening? We'll never know the truth, so I chose the version that best fits the theme of this story: devotion to a sibling.

Readers like you are an inspiration and I'd love to hear from you. Email me anytime at jenni@jenniwiltz.com.

The Natalie Brandon Thrillers

Book 1: The Romanov Legacy
A Murdered Tsar. A Missing Treasure.
One Woman Holds the Key.

Natalie Brandon knows Nicholas II, the last Russian tsar, left behind a secret bank account to provide for his family in exile. But getting someone to believe her is harder than finding the account itself.

Diagnosed with schizophrenia, Natalie is haunted by a recurring hallucination, the voice of an angel named Belial. Even her sister, a history professor, won't take her claim seriously…until a Russian spy kidnaps Natalie, claiming she's the only one who can lead him to the treasure.

But Russia's prime minister, Maxim Starinov, will do anything to get to it first. He joins the deadly hunt, ensnaring Natalie's sister, Constantine's partner, and a loyal Russian family whose only mission is to guard the Romanovs' secret. With her ghostly intuition guiding them, Natalie and Constantine must fight to save the tsar's legacy from a greedy despot.

BOOK 2: THE CARMELITE PROPHECY
A PRICELESS RELIC. A DARING THEFT.
A BLOODLINE REVEALED.

When Natalie Brandon joins her sister Beth in Paris, the past comes alive...and no one escapes unscathed.

Diagnosed with schizophrenia, Natalie is haunted by a recurring hallucination, the voice of an angel named Belial. When he guides her to the church of Saint-Joseph-des-Carmes, Natalie stumbles on two deadly secrets...a family connection to the massacre that took place there during the French Revolution, and a long-lost relic buried deep within its walls.

But Natalie isn't the only one who knows about the relic. An ultra-nationalist French professor steeped in medieval warfare and a former Legionnaire have joined forces to claim the relic and launch an uprising that will end in blood and fire on France's streets. Can Natalie and Beth stay alive long enough to save the relic and stop the next French revolution?

Also by Jenni Wiltz

The Red Road
(literary fiction)

Emma's dad has always promised to send her to college. But when an act of gang violence almost takes his life, Emma can't move on. Will she do what he wants and focus on her own future…or will she jeopardize everything to seek revenge? Available in digital and paperback.

A Vampire in Versailles
(historical horror)

Jean-Gabriel de Bourbon is a vampire whose survival is tied to the French royal family. As long as a king sits on the French throne, Jean-Gabriel lives. But the year is 1788, and the French Revolution draws near. Is anyone, even a vampire, strong enough to stop the force of destiny? Available in digital and paperback.

I Never Arkansas It Coming
(mystery)

Brett Sargent isn't adapting to life in Arkansas very well. A native New Yorker in the Witness Protection Program, she's trying to keep a low profile after testifying against a Mafia up-and-comer. But when a Little Falls truck driver turns up dead with a Mafia calling card stabbed to his chest, Brett knows she's next on their hit list. Available in digital and paperback.

ABOUT THE AUTHOR

Author photo by Ryan Donahue

Jenni Wiltz writes fiction and creative nonfiction. She's won national writing awards for her short fiction, romantic suspense, and creative nonfiction. Her short stories have appeared in *Gargoyle*, the *Portland Review*, and an anthology published by the *Chicago Tribune*. When she's not writing, she enjoys running and genealogical research. She lives in Pilot Hill, California. Visit her online at JenniWiltz.com.

THE BULL-MAN
AND THE GRASSHOPPER

JEAN RICHEPIN (1849-1926) was fined and imprisoned when his first collection of poems, *La Chanson des gueux* (1876) was prosecuted for obscenity. His first collection of prose, *Morts bizarres*, was published in the same year. He became one of the most flamboyant literary Bohemians of the *fin-de-siècle*, to the extent that Sarah Bernhardt—opposite whom he starred in one of his plays—declared that he was a bigger ham than she was. Amazingly, he was elected to the Académie, in a three-cornered contest against Henry de Régnier (who was elected to the next vacant chair) and Edmond Haraucourt. He was one of the most craftsmanlike mass-producers of short fiction for newspaper *feuilleton* slots; a sampler of his work in that vein in translation is *The Crazy Corner: Horrible Stories* (Black Coat Press, 2013).

BRIAN STABLEFORD has been publishing fiction and non-fiction for fifty years. His fiction includes an eighteen-volume series of "tales of the biotech revolution" and a series of half a dozen metaphysical fantasies set in Paris in the 1840s, featuring Edgar Poe's Auguste Dupin. His most recent non-fiction projects are *New Atlantis: A Narrative History of British Scientific Romance* (Wildside Press, 2016) and *The Plurality of Imaginary Worlds: The Evolution of French* roman scientifique (Black Coat Press, 2016); in association with the latter he has translated approximately a hundred and fifty volumes of texts not previously available in English, similarly issued by Black Coat Press.